Mersadez Tanner

The Elite Academy

AF205011

Mersadez Tanner

The Elite Academy

A Novel.

JustFiction Edition

Impressum/Imprint (nur für Deutschland/only for Germany)
Bibliografische Information der Deutschen Nationalbibliothek: Die Deutsche Nationalbibliothek verzeichnet diese Publikation in der Deutschen Nationalbibliografie; detaillierte bibliografische Daten sind im Internet über http://dnb.d-nb.de abrufbar.
Alle in diesem Buch genannten Marken und Produktnamen unterliegen warenzeichen-, marken- oder patentrechtlichem Schutz bzw. sind Warenzeichen oder eingetragene Warenzeichen der jeweiligen Inhaber. Die Wiedergabe von Marken, Produktnamen, Gebrauchsnamen, Handelsnamen, Warenbezeichnungen u.s.w. in diesem Werk berechtigt auch ohne besondere Kennzeichnung nicht zu der Annahme, dass solche Namen im Sinne der Warenzeichen- und Markenschutzgesetzgebung als frei zu betrachten wären und daher von jedermann benutzt werden dürften.

Coverbild: www.ingimage.com

Verlag: JustFiction! Edition ist ein Imprint der
LAP LAMBERT Academic Publishing GmbH & Co. KG
Heinrich-Böcking-Str. 6-8, 66121 Saarbrücken, Deutschland
Telefon +49 681 37 20 310, Telefax +49 681 37 20 310-9
Email: info@justfiction-edition.com

Herstellung in Deutschland:
Schaltungsdienst Lange o.H.G., Berlin
Books on Demand GmbH, Norderstedt
Reha GmbH, Saarbrücken
Amazon Distribution GmbH, Leipzig
ISBN: 978-3-8454-4520-5

Imprint (only for USA, GB)
Bibliographic information published by the Deutsche Nationalbibliothek: The Deutsche Nationalbibliothek lists this publication in the Deutsche Nationalbibliografie; detailed bibliographic data are available in the Internet at http://dnb.d-nb.de.
Any brand names and product names mentioned in this book are subject to trademark, brand or patent protection and are trademarks or registered trademarks of their respective holders. The use of brand names, product names, common names, trade names, product descriptions etc. even without a particular marking in this works is in no way to be construed to mean that such names may be regarded as unrestricted in respect of trademark and brand protection legislation and could thus be used by anyone.

Cover image: www.ingimage.com

Publisher: JustFiction! Edition
is an imprint of the publishing house
LAP LAMBERT Academic Publishing GmbH & Co. KG
Heinrich-Böcking-Str. 6-8, 66121 Saarbrücken, Germany
Phone +49 681 37 20 310, Fax +49 681 37 20 310-9
Email: info@justfiction-edition.com

Printed in the U.S.A.
Printed in the U.K. by (see last page)
ISBN: 978-3-8454-4520-5

Table of Contents

To those I love,

"Believe in me, just keep your faith and believe in all that you make.
Believe in me, my love is not a gamble.
You can count on me."

-Blood on the Dance Floor. "Believe."
Epic. Candyland Records, 2010.

"I will be there!
I will always be there!"

-Black Veil Brides. "Savior."
Set the World On Fire. Lava Records, 2011.

{1} WELCOME HOME

I arrived on campus feeling like the innocent little 16 year old that I was pretending not to be. My parents hadn't been particularly pleased when I told them about this opportunity, but high school just wasn't the place for me anymore. It was that beige envelope that arrived just three short months ago that landed me here in this hot, muggy, dying town. It was in the middle of nowhere Alabama and the only thing worth mentioning was Forrestine University.

Forrestine University. A university made up of three academic buildings, the main Union, and two dormitories. The campus was nothing like the struggling town that lingered just outside its gates. In town, yards were made up of dirt with the occasional dried up hydrangea bush. But here, the grounds were pristine, with lush green grass that had been trimmed perfectly, almost as if every blade had been cut by hand. Off in the distance I could see the fountain that represented the heart of Forrestine. I'd give anything right now to just make a run for that fountain and jump in.

But I couldn't. I had to wait for the campus guide that was to escort me to my new dorm and give me the itinerary for the next week. This guide was already ten minutes late, and I felt like my favorite orange tank top was about to reach up and strangle me. I'd brought my car with me, but since I didn't have a parking pass yet, I had decided to lug my luggage bags up to the meeting point. Not my best idea ever. I pulled out my i-Pod, Kesha started singing about some loser being a stupid boy as they usually are. This set me off, thinking about everything that had happened this past year.

They say you can tell when a girl has been hurt because she will change how she looks. In my case, this was most definitely true. I lost weight, dyed my hair a luscious dark brown, wore contacts, and now garnered an attitude that could rival the best of them. I used to be a shy girl, when we'd moved to a new town in sixth grade it took me a whole year just to make one friend. Once I did we were inseparable.

If I had to describe Liz-Beth in three words, they would be outgoing, awkward, and clumsy. She made it her goal to make sure everyone around her felt included, a personality contrary to the assumption her flaming red hair would give her. With her on my side, my friends continued to grow. Until sophomore year that is. It all changed overnight, we had been partying with our new friends, a couple senior boys, and the next thing I knew, they hated me. With the snap of a finger, five girls turned on me with out a second thought.

That had only been ten months ago, but I had changed so much. I went through a horrible fight with depression. I kept it to myself though, not wanting anyone to know how week I really was. Eventually I pulled past the cutting, I made sure no one knew it had ever happened and hid the scars behind my edgy new style. Never leaving my room without a bandana firmly secured on my wrist. One night, as I was lying in my bed, the room started feeling stuffy and I just had to get out. That's how I stumbled across my next release. It was a house party. I'd never actually gone out and partied but when I was invited in, I decided to try it. It was a risk to go in alone, but that's what I needed, that's what I craved. Time was lost on me then. Well, almost. The day I got the invitation was the day I stopped.

Fast forward to now. Standing outside the gates of Forrestine, waiting to be escorted to my future at the Elite Academy. Students were selected based on academic potential, boy were they going to be disappointed when they got my grades. The only information I'd had about the academy was what they sent to my mailbox. As far as Google was concerned, the Elite Academy didn't even exist.

"Ahh, You must be Carisma Larson."

I glanced over the top of my aviators to see a boy not much older than myself. He was wearing dark wash jeans and a polo that fit tight in all the right places. I had no idea how he managed in this heat, but I suppose it was to look professional and such. He had golden brown hair that glistened in the sun and looked like he'd just gotten out of bed. Somehow he made it look sexy though. Doing a quick once-over, I noticed that his arms...no scratch that; his entire body...was toned to perfection. Not in the overdone bodybuilder way, but if we were betting in the ring, my money would be on him. Easily. I pushed myself off the pillar I was leaning against while offering my hand to introduce myself.

"Please, call me Carrie. And who might I be speaking to?" I smiled while shaking the stranger's hand, and looked up to meet his eyes, which were a piercing blue-grey. I'd never seen eyes like his before, but what I had seen before was the look in them. I recognized it from my own eyes; it was one of the saddest things you could see in a person. Emptyness. I'd woken up passed out in my bathroom, when I looked at myself in the mirror, my eyes held nothing. They were empty tunnels echoing the defeat I felt. I wanted to know what happened to make this seemingly perfect boy so exhausted and hopeless.

"Umm...Oh right... Umm... Mason Bethesda." Thank god, I didn't think the boy was ever going to spit out his name.

"Well, It's wonderful to meet you Mason! How about we find my dorm?" The sun was beating down, and the hot gusts of wind were making me all the more ready to be welcomed by some crisp clean air conditioned air.

"Of course, so what kind of stuff do you like to do for fun?" He surprisingly didn't stutter as we grabbed my suitcases. I guess it was just a one-time fault.

I thought back to the last time I went out. My class was renowned for the kick ass bonfires the student council put together. Unofficially, of course. Like everyone, I was having an amazing time drinking and drowning my problems away. Out of nowhere, the schools state ranked defensive tackle, Chuck, had come up behind me.

"You're really, really, really pretty. Why haven't I ever noticed you before babe?" Chuck's words were slurring together and he stagnant odor of cheap beer poured off of him.

The way he was trying to run his hands all over me didn't catch anyone's attention since we were on the makeshift dance floor. I turned around, letting us face each other and making it easier for me to push him away.

"Very cute, problem is you really, really, really aren't my type," I said, turning away from him. I couldn't help mimicking him with my own sarcastic tone.

"That's not very nice." His voice was suddenly laced with anger.

Before I could get away from Chuck, he grabbed my wrist and began to drag me backwards, towards the woods surrounding the area. With the echoing of the music, my screams went unheard into the night. I started clawing at his arm with my nails, hoping to loosen his grip. It didn't work.

8

"By the time I'm done with you, you'll know how to treat someone that compliments you," and with that he slammed me into the nearest tree.

I could feel the bark piercing my skin. This couldn't be happening. Not to me. I tried to twist and fight my way out of his hold, but in seconds he was yanking my jaw to where he wanted it. There wasn't anything I could do.

With all the will left in me, I took the beer bottle that was still in my hand and slammed it on Chuck's head. Glass flew everywhere, and his concentration broke just enough I was able to tear away from him. I made my way through the trees, tears running down my face, looking for the clearing that served as a parking lot. Finding my car, I was home free. It was the first time I drove drunk, and the last time I went alone to a party.

"I like to have a good time, interpret that as you please." Immediately, Mason was trying to hide a smirk, making me laugh. I knew he was probably thinking I must be some easy party slut, but he was wrong. I had learned the games that boys play, and then I played it better.

"Well, you'll have to come out with me and some friends sometime. You're at the state's premier party school, which you probably already know." He joked at the schools reputation. When my parents discovered where the academy was located, they weren't even going to consider letting me come. I bombarded them with the parent information book, which they finally read and must have liked something because here I was.

"Maybe I will." I said this knowing I most likely never would. I'd promised myself when I came here that I wouldn't go out and get trashed on the weekends, but that didn't mean I couldn't hang out with friends.

"Carrie, I would like to welcome you to Marshall Hall, as well as the Elite Academy. I am what the officials here would call your 'Senior Mentor.'" Shocker! He knew I was part of the Elite Academy, which prided itself on secrecy even within this bustling college environment. At least that's what the invitation had said.

"Hmm, does that mean I'll be seeing you a lot?" I smiled thinking about the possibilities. He must have taken it the wrong way though.

"Have I really been that horrible my first day on the job?" He laughed nervously at the end of his question.

"Definitely not! It'll be nice to know one person here, even if I am just your job." I gave him a smile that I only hoped didn't look as stupid as I felt. It was the best answer I could come up with; I couldn't exactly say 'I want to know so that I'll look sexy whenever you see me.'

"Awesome, but I don't need to be paid to hang out with you. This is as far as I go," he says handing me a set of keys, "one opens the building doors after business hours, and the other is your room key. Go through the doors and to your right will be an elevator, third floor, fifth door on the right. Your roommate has already arrived."

I looked up at the building I would be living in for the next two years. It was probably fifteen stories tall, and was built in the collegiate gothic style. I could see up to the very top where a bell town hung prominently. Hopefully they didn't actually use it. If I had to guess, I'd say the building was at least one hundred years old.

"Why is-," but Mason was already gone. I swear I hadn't been looking up for more than two seconds, and yet he was nowhere in sight.

Well, it's now or never. I followed Mason's directions absently until I was standing in front of my door. I suddenly felt a lot of pressure, knowing my new roommate was on the other side of the door. They say first impressions are the most important, and I kept my fingers crossed that this one was good. I slid the key in the lock, turned it, and walked into my new home.

I walked into room 325. It was huge for what I'd imagined a dorm room being. There were closets on each side of the door, and against the wall was a dresser with a mirror attached. On the left side of the room were two desks facing each other, I would be so strange studying there, I'd constantly feel like someone was watching me. On the right side of the room was a set of bunk beds.

I noticed there were a bunch of duffel bags laid across the top bunk. This brought me back to reality. I turned towards the closet where a shuffling noise was coming from, and sure enough, there was my roommate. She had her iPod on full blast, and it looked like the closet was trying to eat her. It was packed with clothes and shoes. I would have completely missed her if her leg hadn't been about to knock a bunch of hair stuff off the dresser.

"Ahhh," she screamed as a bottle went flying off the dresser. I caught it right before it hit the ground.

"Hey, I'm Carisma," I said as I handed the bottle of 'Big Sexy Hair' hair spray back to her. I looked up at her, and lets just say the bottle definitely described her hair. She had platinum blonde curls that went down past her shoulder blades. She was a size 2 at the most, making me feel like an elephant. Not to mention she had a huge chest, there was no way that was natural. Weird, my parents would have murdered me if I had ever wanted plastic surgery.

"Hi, I was wondering when you would get here. I can't wait, this year is going to be so fun! I have so much planned for us! Oh, I really, really wanted the top bunk, so I figured I'd let you have the better closet, its got shelves in it for shoes and stuff, plus I'm not very organized so it wouldn't be any use to me anyways."

Her mouth was like the energizer bunny. "Oh, and my name is Sadie Porter." The smile she plastered on her face seemed to fit with her. Even though I hadn't talked to her much, I could tell that she was a bubbly, cheery, happy person. We were definitely polar opposites.

"Thanks for the closet, and I was hoping for the bottom bunk anyways. I have a fear of falling, lame I know." She talked...ALOT, but hopefully she isn't one of those ditzy girls whose only care in the world is guys. Don't get me wrong, boys are fun toys, but I just don't think you should get so attached that you're life completely revolves around them.

"Have you seen all the amazing guys around here?" There goes that hope. "I've yet to see one that didn't have at least a six-pack. Of course I've only seen Elite guys so far. I can't believe they live on the same floor as us. I mean its so weird, no other school would ever let that happen, because you know we're just hormonal teenagers waiting to jump each other. Oh, wait, that's exactly what we are!" Did the girl always talk so much? She started with looking at boys and ended with jumping their bones.

"Well, so far I've only met my 'senior mentor,'" I said that with the finger quotes, " what's with that anyways, why do we need to follow a senior around?"

"I'm not sure what that's about, but I got Evelyn Rooks. She's freakin' scary! She didn't say more than three words to me. I wonder if the girls get paired with girls and boys with boys," I laughed when she said this, "who did you get paired with?"

I had a sneaking suspicion she wasn't going to like my answer, "Mason Bethesda."

"Ohmegee! No fair! Why did I get the evil bitch and you get the hot boy? Ugg, this is not fair! I have to go call daddy. Humph!" She stormed out of the room, the door slamming behind her. Thankfully no one else was in the room to see my face as I stood there with my mouth wide open, which had to look stupid. Boy crazy I could deal with, but spoiled brat with entitlement issues...no way!

I started unpacking my stuff. I was scary organized, at least when it came to my clothes. Everyone that knew me was used to this. Shorts, pants, and dress pants had to be separated. In the last two drawers went underwear and pajama clothes. In the closet went my shirts, separating t-shirts from my cute tops.

In the bottom of my closet were a bunch of boxes. Grr...and here I thought I was done unpacking. I forgot that my parents had me pack all my stuff, other than clothes, in these brown boxes and we had them shipped here last week. I had my huge Roxy book bag hiding out in the back of the closet somewhere too.

When I'd finally finished putting stuff away, I collapsed on my bed and looked at my finished product. My desk had been adorned with red and black desk organizing things. There was the red lamp next to the mini set of drawers and on the opposite side of the desk was a black paper tray and red pencil jar. I had put up pictures all around my bed, desk, and dresser. They reminded me of fun times, better times. My bed was plain and simple, white sheets and a black comforter. Just then there was a knock at the door. Weird, Sadie must have forgotten her key in her haste to call daddy.

"So what'd daddy have to say about the hot boy mentors?" I said as I opened the door. Bad idea!

Standing in front of me was possibly the hottest guy I have ever laid eyes on. He had short black hair, and deadly golden brown eyes. I was afraid if he narrowed his eyes just right, I'd just have to lie down and die. He gave off a vibe that made you convinced that you would do anything to stay as far away from his bad side as possible. He was wearing a tight black t-shirt; I'd be lying if I said I wasn't imagining what was underneath it. His jeans fit perfectly, like they were made just for him. The hem of his t-shirt rested just on a shiny black belt buckle, "Cocky." Oh crap, I think I've been checking him out way too long, I wonder if he noticed.

"I don't know about daddy, but I think you should stay away from those hot boy mentors, I would prefer to keep you all to myself," he said with a smirk, making a wave of heat coursing through my body. Nevertheless, I was shocked. Did these boys normally talk like this around here? Either way, I think it's safe to say that his belt buckle is described him to the letter.

"Very funny, but I do the playing, not the other way around. Can I help you with something," I winced, realizing my bad choice of words.

He raised an eyebrow, "Well there are many things you could help me with doll, but we'll save that for later. I'm your new mentor; I'll be taking over for Mason. Be in these at 0500 tomorrow," he said while chucking a plain black duffel bag at me, "Oh and you have a meeting with the headmaster at 1400 today. Have fun!" Huh?

"Wait, what? Why are you taking over for Mason? And what do you mean 1400? Don't call me doll!" What the heck is going on? I was so confused, and it didn't help that the whole time he was talking I ended up staring at his lips.

"Army time, babe, get used to it." He said gliding down the hall and disappearing from sight.

What the hell? I didn't know I was signing up for the army when I came here. I would never put up with any of my peers bossing me around, and yes, this includes my "mentor." I still don't know why we need them, but whatever. I haven't decided yet, but I might be okay with seeing my new mentor more often. As he walked down the hallway and disappeared, I checked him out, and unfortunately I liked it more than I should have.

I opened the duffel bag he'd thrown at me and saw it was full of clothes. Judging by the type of clothing, I was in for a workout tomorrow. Oh jeez, at five in the morning no less. I was one of those girls that functioned best sleeping until at least ten, but because of school, I had perfected the art of getting ready in fifteen minutes or less. This maximized my sleeping time and, in my opinion, made me a much more pleasant person throughout the day.

He said something about a meeting with Headmaster Morgon, I'm guessing in his office. I don't even know where that is and the meeting is in ten minutes! After I had accepted my invitation to the academy, Headmaster Morgon had come to my house and visited with my parents. I didn't know all of what they discussed, but I remember walking in the door from school and hearing him say "she's the most promising of our new class and I will personally make sure that she is trained by the best," which didn't make sense to me, but I didn't really dwell on it. I was going to school, learning, not training.

I took a quick look through the folder that had been sitting on my desk when I'd arrived. It said the headmaster's office was in this building, on the thirteenth floor, but it didn't give a room number. Oh well, if I got up to the thirteenth floor, then I'd at least be closer than I was now. I walked towards the elevator that I'd taken up here just a few hours before. To my dismay, there was a bright pink sign,

Elevator out of service. Stairs are at the opposite end of the hallway. Sorry for the inconvenience.

I glanced at my watch, six minutes, now I really would have to make a run for it. Off I went, hoping that no one got in my way. This was surely an accident waiting to happen.

When I finally got to the thirteenth floor, I looked at my watch. I still had a minute left. I pushed the heavy metal door open, leaving the stairwell. Surprisingly, there wasn't a hallway, just a set of oak doors that had to be at least ten feet high.

As if on cue the doors opened revealing an older gentleman, weird, he was dressed as a butler, but I had the feeling he could transform into James Bond in the blink of an eye.

The room I stepped into was massive and empty. All it contained was a desk and chair that looked like they were meant for a king. Seated in the throne was a man that appeared to be in his early thirties. He had light blond hair that was spiked up in all directions. His attire was a startling contrast to his hair. His suit looked like it was designer brand and tailor to fit only him. This was Headmaster Morgon. He was already speaking to someone. When they noticed the door open, they went silent. As I approached, I could tell it was Him. The incredibly hot boy also known as my new "mentor." He was standing with his feet shoulder-width apart and his hands rested on his lower back. He reminded me of a soldier with his attentiveness and look of pure, unwavering, focus.

I walked up beside him and faced Headmaster Morgon, mimicking his pose.

"Ah, Ms. Larson, I'm glad you could join us. Mr. Tandem was just about to explain to me why he didn't escort you here himself as he should have. However, since you've arrived, I insist that we skip that matter for now and get on to the more pressing issues." I could see Tandem shift his weight slightly at Morgon's insult. Seems to me like someone wasn't doing his job very well. Ha, burn!

"Ms. Larson, you have been selected as one of the elite of the elite. Unfortunately for you, you will have to earn more information. And that will come at the discretion of Mr. Tandem, who you will begin training tomorrow. You will continue until he is satisfied that you have met the requirements." Huh?

"While I'm honored Headmaster Morgon, what do you mean 'elite of the elite' and what are the requirements for?" Tandem elbowed me in the ribs. "Ow!" I whispered.

"That is not of your concern right now Ms. Larson, all you need to know at this point is that Mr. Tandem is your mentor, your instructor. He will help you in your classes, push you father physically than you've ever been before, and for all intensive purposes, he is your boss. I expect you to treat him as such." What was that supposed to mean? "You are both excused, I'll be expecting that report at the end of the week Mr. Tandem."

"Yes, sir," Tandem said, then turned on his heal and began to leave the room. I followed him, listening as my steps echoed on the marble floor. He had the answers I wanted; now I just had to get them from him. When we finally reached the tall oak doors half a century later, Butler 007 swung them open releasing us from the Headmaster's chambers.

"Hey," I said as soon as the doors were shut. He kept walking on. He ignored me. That pissed me off. The least he could say was buzz off or something like that.

"I was talking to you." I grabbed his arm and tried to get him to face me, but I couldn't. Of course, I couldn't help but notice the muscle that pulsed under the flimsy t-shirt he was in.

"I know," he said, suddenly grabbing my arm and pulling me into the stairwell. Before I knew what had happened, he had shoved me into the wall and positioned himself so that he had one leg on each side of mine. I could feel his warm breath roll over my cheek, causing a shiver to roll through my body. It was then that I realized just how close we were, if it weren't for our clothes, I'd be at risk for pregnancy.

"Now what was it that you wanted?" His voice emanated danger, and I was almost too scared to look up.

But being me, I did. I'd never let anyone see that kind of emotion. I locked eyes with him, and noticed that, like Mason, his eyes appeared empty. However, his seemed more like pseudo-emptiness, like he'd put up this barrier between him and the world. A deadly poker face.

"What's your name?" I started with a simple enough question, hoping my own poker face didn't show how uncomfortable and nervous he was actually making me.

Suddenly he was on the move again, making his way towards the steps, "Kain. Kain Tandem."

"I wasn't done," I finally yelled as he practically ran down the stairs, but I heard a door slam shut and knew he didn't hear.

Wow, what a jerk. I can't believe he slammed me up against the wall. It took me a minute in the stairwell just to get my heart to slow down. Kain was definitely dangerous, I could just tell by the look in his eyes.

When I finally felt normal again, I made my way back to my room, praying that Sadie was still away crying to daddy. To my dismay, she was back in our room putting on what very well might be her third coat of eye make up today. I normally wouldn't be this mean to someone, but there's just something about her. Kain probably isn't really helping my attitude either. At least I keep it all in my head.

"Ugg, daddy won't do anything! I'm stuck with Evelyn! I can't believe he could do this. He calls it punishment but really it's just his sick idea of torture. I don't know why he's still punishing me for the accident. I mean wasn't it bad enough that he took away my credit cards and made me leave my school for this hell hole." She doesn't even care whom she's talking to, she just speaks to hear her voice.

"Well life just became fair. Mason isn't my mentor anymore." I said collapsing on my bed.

"Ooo, why not?" This new information perked her up.

"I have no idea, but my new mentor, Kain, is probably a psychotic serial killer in his spare time." That was scary to imagine. Not to mention the fact that I was going to have to work with him a lot from the sound of it.

"So they took you away from one cute guy, put you with a new cute guy, one that gets way more points on the hot scale if he's really the bad boy you claim he is, and your complaining? You, my dear Carisma, are insane!" Oh, wow, I forgot to tell her I go be Carrie.

I hate the name Carisma. It makes me feel like I should be happy and smiley all the time, and that's just not me. My name is the complete opposite of my personality. I'm usually in this scary self-destructive mode where all I want to do is have fun, party, and pretty much not care about the world, or the future, or anything that I know I should care about.

"I go by Carrie, I guess I forgot to tell you earlier. And Kain is not the sexy bad boy type of dangerous. He's more like the death row serial killer type. Prison is not hot." As the words came out of my mouth, I knew I was lying to Sadie and myself. That boy was a freakin' god.

Sure, I wasn't kidding the whole serial-killer thing, but I could handle him. I think.

"Right I bet he is, and bunnies are really vampires in disguise. Daddy would never let a 'psychotic serial killer' into Elite." No way! Her dad was Headmaster Morgon. At least he wasn't a push over or she'd be ruling this school.

"Your dad is Headmaster Morgon?" I asked, needing to be sure of my assumptions.

"Yeah, really he's my step-dad, but he's raised me since I was like three, so same diff right? Anyways, I am so excited for tomorrow! First day of classes, older college boys, it's going to be so fun! I have to pick out my outfit. What are you going to wear?" Well at least there's something we have in common.

I love clothes! Sure, I'll admit sometimes I dress like a slut, but I'm not one. Maybe slut is too harsh, daring might be a better word. I'm still a virgin and I've never had an actual boyfriend. The farthest I've gone with a boy is making out, and that was just the Derrick. I shivered just thinking about it, I was such a stupid freshman. He was possibly the nastiest kisser ever; it was like making out with a giant slobbery bulldog. I don't think making out with a dog should count as a first kiss, so I don't count it.

"That's cool. I haven't decided what I'm wearing yet, but I'm thinking a skirt and tank. Oh, and my stripper boots." They weren't really stripper boots, but the heals were nearly four inches. I could pull them off without looking freakishly tall with my tiny 5'3" stature.

"Sexy! I'm going to wear my pink dress. It's my favorite! Uh oh," she said, checking her watch, "I forgot I'm supposed to be having dinner with daddy, see you later!" With that she was gone. I had a feeling this girl wore a lot of pink. Ick, guess I'm going to have to get used to it. I'm okay with pink, but I always pair it with black so I don't blind anyone with the brightness.

I decided to curl up in my bed for a while and listen to my i-Pod before I went to dinner. I was thinking about everything that had happened today and the new people I've met. My roommate was a boy-crazy spoiled brat, but I could probably get along with her well enough to live with her. Mason was nice and I hope I'll get to see him again. Then there was my replacement mentor, Kain. I could already tell that getting along with him was going to be nearly impossible. I have issues with authority, and by issues, I mean I hate people telling me what to do as well as people ignoring me. We were going to be butting heads at every turn.

Before I knew it, my eyes were drifting shut and my thoughts left me.

I could feel my phone vibrating somewhere. Ugg, and I was just getting to the really good part of my dream. I was partying it out on stage with 3Oh!3, It was pitch black in my room, and what the hell is that noise?

It was Sadie snoring...great.

I finally found my phone under my pillow. I looked at it without even thinking. Worst idea ever! It's like looking at the sun, only worse because you've been in pitch dark.

It was 1:32 in the morning, or as Kain would say, "0132 hours...grr!" I don't think he'd really say grr, but hey, it's my imagination. It was a text that had woken me up, but I didn't recognize the number it belonged to.

"Hey, meet me on the first floor lobby ASAP!"

Yeah right! There's no way I'm leaving my room in the middle of the night to meet a stranger in an empty place that I'm not familiar with. What kind of idiot does this person think I am?

I decided to reply, just to see who it was.

"Who is this?"

It wasn't even thirty seconds before I got another text.

"Mason, hurry up!"

This better be important! I was only getting out of my super comfy bed because it was Mason, and he was really nice to me yesterday. And also, I'm hoping that maybe he'll be able to tell me why he was replaced with Kain as my mentor.

I definitely wasn't going out side. That would require getting warmer clothes on, which would risk waking up the lumberjack. I was in bright yellow soffe shorts with a white and black zebra print tank top. I know, I sport some fierce sleepwear. I put on my Roxy slippers that were by the door and slipped out into the hall.

Just then my phone vibrated again,

"Watch for hall sweeps."

Wow, he could have mentioned that before I left my room. There was probably a pattern to hall sweeps, the most of which would be every fifteen minutes. It was now 1:37, so I might have around eight minutes to get downstairs to the lobby. That was plenty of time, but I decided to make a run for the stairwell just in case.

I was almost to the stairwell when I heard voices on the other side of the door. Crap, what do I do now, there's no way I'll make it back to my room. I took a chance and grabbed the nearest doorknob, which luckily wasn't locked. Slipping inside, I pressed myself into the nearest wall as if the voices would somehow be able to see through the door.

"What are you doing?" That was not the voice I wanted to hear right now. I turned around and was face-to-face with Kain.

"Umm...sleepwalking," I said, throwing out the first excuse that came to mind. It wasn't supposed to sound like a question though. This was not going to have a good ending.

"Sure you were, babe. I'll make you a deal." These pet names were going to get old fast. I didn't see any way to get out of this other than to take his deal. It was a risk I had to take.

"...and the deal is?" The look on his face was making me nervous. I felt like I was being eye-raped, but hopefully I was just imagining that. Well, on second thought, it might not be so bad. Wait, what am I thinking, this is wrong on so many levels. This was only going to get me in trouble.

"I'll let you go back to...sleepwalking...and I'll collect at a later date. Accept?" He stuck his hand out to shake on it.

"That's not fair. I'm not going to blindly agree to perverted thing you come up with."

"Well, I'd be more than happy to do my job and call Headmaster Morgon to see what he wants to do with you." What the heck, if it'll get me out of trouble now, I'll deal with the consequences later.

I grabbed his hand, "Deal." Maybe I was imagining it, but wherever his skin was in contact with mine, it felt like flames were licking the surface.

"Good. Sweeps are done for the night anyways," he chucked. I let go of his hand and slipped back out the door I came in.

As soon as I got out of there, I took off running down to the lobby. Mason was waiting when I walked in, pacing back and forth.

"Geez, it took you long enough. Did ASAP and hurry up not register?" Wow, what was his problem.

"God, don't be a bitch Mason. I had to make a deal with the devil to get away from the sweeps. What was so important that it couldn't wait till, oh, I don't know, daylight!?" I swear if this isn't important I might strangle him. I dragged myself out of bed, went through all that mess, and he wants to act like a douche.

"Your right, I'm sorry. Don't hate me, but what I'm going to tell you isn't going to seem important at all right now, and I can't tell you this all at once because you'd forget half of it. This school isn't a normal school for all the students. It's different for some." This was not life threatening, world-ending, worthy-of-crawling-out-of-bed information.

"Right, its some kind of army school training an legion of genius soldiers. Why aren't you my mentor anymore?" I hoped my sarcasm showed that I was thinking the way he was acting made him seem slightly crazy.

"Ha, army school. This place couldn't be further away from government sanctions," that was supposed to be a joke, "I'm not considered fit for duty any longer since..."

I waited for him to finish his thought, but instead he just shook his head and got this totally spaced out look. Finally, I shook his shoulder, hoping it would snap him out of whatever trance he was in. It seemed to work because he came back and put his hands over his eyes, shaking his head. Weird.

"What duty are you not fit for?" I asked, knowing he probably wouldn't answer, but it was worth a shot.

"I've already told you more than I should have. Tandem is good at what he does, but he's really harsh. Just don't let him get to you and watch who you trust." So, is he telling me to trust Kain or not, or is he talking about everyone? Its way too late, or early, for this kind of conversation.

30

I didn't say anything, I wanted to wait for him to change his mind and tell me what was going on. No use, he was done.

"You should get back to your room, you have to be up in two hours."

"Okay, got it, I'm going!" Bi-polar much? At any moment he might start pulling his hair out.

The trip back to my room went smoothly, and when I got there Sadie was still passed out. Geez, the girl couldn't even be quiet in her sleep!

I looked at my phone. It was already past two in the morning, and I had to be up in three hours. This was going to be an awesome day... not!

"Ahhh!" I tried to scream when the cold sensation hit me, but before any sound escaped a hand was clamped over my mouth. What was happening? It felt like I had just dunked my head in a freezing pool.

All the sudden, the water was shut off, but it was still dark. My clothes were soaked! What the heck? "Umph," I was still sitting at the bottom of the open shower when something hit me in the gut. I heard footsteps walking away from me, and then with the flip of a switch, the lights came on. It took me a few seconds to get used to the blinding light, but when my eyes finally adjusted, there was Kain.

Crap! I was supposed to be ready at five.

"Put these on now. It'd be wise of you to remember that when I say 0500, I mean 0500," he glanced at his watch, "not 0504." You've got to be kidding me. In four minutes he had decided I wasn't up, kidnapped me from my room, and threw me in this shower for a hellish wake up call. Lame.

"I'm not getting dressed with you in here, perv."

"Don't worry, I'll having you stripping at my command before long." I waited for him to leave and shut the door behind him.

I opened the duffel bag and put on the clothes that were in it: spandex short-shorts, I don't think I've ever seen shorts this short, long pants, white socks which luckily were no-shows since any other kind bothers me, Nike running shoes, a sports bra, and a windbreaker.

All of it was black. Don't get me wrong, I love wearing black, but not this much. There is such a thing as overdoing it. Anyways, I looked around the bathroom I was in. It wasn't one of the giant shared bathrooms that we were supposed to use. The counter was full of guy stuff, shaving cream and axe. No fair! He totally has his own bathroom. Suddenly there was a pounding on the door.

"Hurry the hell up Carisma, you've got seven minutes to make up for!" Today was not going to go well, he was already being Mr. Bossy Pants. I quickly threw all my wet clothes in the duffel bag and walked out of the bathroom.

"It's Carrie, and just so you know, I hate you." I didn't usually tell people I hated them, but the disgusting smirk he had on when I came out of the bathroom justified it. Of course, any other time that smirk would have made me melt, but not after waking up to a cold shower.

"You know you love me babe, and you might try not sleepwalking so much. I think it's interfering with your sleep and my schedule." He said as he put his arm around my shoulders and ushered me towards the door.

"Keep your hands to yourself," I shrugged his arm off me. He's probably used to getting what he wants. By what, I mean who.

"What are we doing anyways?" I yawned after I said this. I already feel exhausted and the workout hasn't even started.

"Today I'm going to gage your endurance, 5 miles in 30 minutes." He was dressed similar to me, but as soon as we stepped outside, he took his shirt off, tucking it into the waistband of his pants.

"Are you ready?" He was looking straight at me. I'm sure I had a deer-in-the-headlights look. Kain was ripped. From what I could see he had an eight-pack and his arms were huge. I was so distracted, I didn't notice when he stepped over to me, standing way too close for comfort.

He started to worry me as he leaned down towards my neck.

"Beat me and I'll show you more," he whispered so close to my ear that I think I could feel his lips. This brought me back to reality.

"No thanks, if I beat you, put your clothes back on perv," I know that's the exact opposite of what I wanted, but I was scared of what anything with him could lead to. With that I took off running, I knew he'd catch up with me easily, but I was pacing myself.

He stayed at my pace, even though I'm pretty sure he could've gone a lot faster and beat me easy. He was probably setting us up for an all out sprint at the end.

"Five miles at the fountain, good luck sweetheart." He laughed, while pointing to a fountain no more than 100 meters in front of us. He had started picking up his pace, leaving me behind. I decided to take advantage of his ignorance, and picked up my own pace so that I was behind him, but just out of site. Hopefully he didn't turn around and ruin my plan.

He still hadn't looked when I made my move. I broke into an all out sprint for the fountain. There was no way I was gonna let him win.

"Hey!" I heard him yell from, at the most, five feet behind me. It didn't matter it was already too late. I jumped into the fountain and felt the cool water on my legs. I put my hands on my knees and leaned over to catch my breath. Now, I'd be perfectly content to be back in that cold shower.

I climbed out of the fountain. The sun hadn't even risen yet. This was an ungodly hour to be up, but at least it was a nice run…and, I guess, adequate company. I walked up to Kain.

"Aww is someone a sore loser? I know what would make it better." I started to put my hands on his hips as he took the bait and put his arms around me, resting his hands on my lower back.

"I might have an idea of what you could do to make it better." He whispered as he pulled me to him. Ha! Yeah right! I grabbed his t-shirt from where it was in his waistband and shoved it into his chest.

"Loser, put your clothes on!" I yelled back to him as I took off towards the dorm for a much-needed shower.

Luckily Kain hadn't locked the door in his rush to kidnap me in my sleep. It was still dark outside and according to my phone it wasn't even six yet. I knew we were supposed to get our schedule from our academic advisor before eight, so I had awhile to get ready.

I took my towel off the hook in the closet, got out of my nasty sweaty clothes and wrapped the towel around me. I grabbed my shower caddy and slipped out the door to the communal bathroom. Sadie was still asleep, just like everyone else on our floor. Well, at least I'd get to have my pick of the showers.

There were five showers, four of which were at most two feet by two feet. Basically, they were torture boxes for those like me that were claustrophobia. The last shower was massive. It had etched glass doors and three different showerheads. It was like showering in the light rain, weird.

The water felt amazing after that run. This had to be the longest shower of my life. I was just rinsing my hair when I heard the door open, which startled me. I wasn't expecting any of the girls to be up yet.

"Who the fuck is in my shower?" Wow, I was not expecting that. Someone clearly woke up on the wrong side of the bed. If this girl wanted to act like a bitch, I could do the same.

"Who the fuck is asking?" I finished conditioning my hair and stepped out of the shower into the freezing air. I guess I took a really hot shower. I again wrapped my towel around me, got a hair tie and put my hair in a bun, grabbed my shower stuff and stepped out of the changing area.

Standing there, hand on hip, was a girl that was slightly taller than myself. She had light brown curly hair that was going everywhere and she looked pissed. The stench of stale alcohol was rolling off her in waves and she was still wearing yesterday's smeared makeup. You could definitely tell what she did last night.

"So you're one of the new girls. I'll forgive this slip up since you don't know how it works around here. You do what I want, when I want, and get me what I want if asked." I decided just to smile when she said this.

"I think I'll pass." Her jaw dropped, she clearly wasn't used to people denying her wishes, sort of like Sadie. I turned to leave the bathroom.

"Do you know who I am? You don't get to say no to me." No matter how this turned out, I was sure we were going to be enemies.

"No I don't know who you are, and to be honest I don't really care." I said as I pulled the heavy wood door so I could go back to my room and get dressed for the day.

"I'm Evelyn Rooks, ask around." I heard her say as the door slammed shut.

That was Sadie's mentor. Those two were a match made in hell that's for sure.

It was after 6:30 when I got back to my room, and surprisingly Sadie was actually up. I started straightening my hair. It wasn't anywhere near curly, but I liked it best after I ran a straightener through it.

When I finished with my hair I put on my outfit for the day. I decided to wear tight grey leggings that went down to my calves. It was like a second skin, but with all the running I did, my legs could pull it off. Next was the black tank top that hit at the top of my thighs along with the adorable grey vest that went down to the bottom of my rib cage. I opted out of my stripper boots and instead went with a pair of velvety black ankle boots. They had four-inch heels, a mini accent belt that wrapped low, and came to a point at the toe. Perfect ass kicking boots if the need arose.

I threw on my necklace; it was a cross on a thick silver chain. My grandmother had given it to me for my 16th birthday. I quickly put on some eyeliner and mascara, the only make up I used, and I was ready to start the day.

I grabbed my book bag and keys, giving myself an once-over in the full-length mirror on the back of our door. I looked hot, but you'd never catch me in something like this at home. I was always in jeans and a t-shirt, making no attempt whatsoever to show the curves I had. Unless of course I was at a party, but I can almost guarantee you none of those kids knew who I was at school. My parents might cringe if they saw the new me, but I had started over and it was time for changes.

Checking the time on my phone, I decided to head down to the dining hall for a quick breakfast. I had an hour before I could get my schedule. The dining hall was private to Elite Academy, located in the basement of Marshall Hall. Yogurt and granola seemed like the healthiest meal I could get out of there, which was fine by me. I usually didn't eat a whole lot.

The actual dining hall was completely vacant. The carpeting was a deep emerald green with gold accents and matching draperies adorned the walls. Sitting at the nearest table, with my back to a wall, I sank into the exquisite leather chair. I zoned out for a while, just thinking about the possibilities of what was to come this year. Before I knew it, my phone was chiming, telling me it was time to go get my schedule.

I made my way down to the office, where my advisor was. All I knew was that I was going to be in "advanced classes." Hopefully there weren't going to put me in some insane class like quantum physics. Just the thought made me cringe.

When I arrived in the office, the secretary ushered me down a long narrow hallway. At any moment I was expecting the lights to start flickering and the floor to shake. At the end was the office of Dr. Winslow Beckett, my academic advisor. He sounded like a bucket full of joy. Just as I was about to knock on the door, it opened, revealing a man that couldn't be more than 35.

"There you are Carisma, or, I'm sorry, Carrie, I'm Dr. Winslow Beckett. I hate to just rush off but I have a meeting to get to, here's your schedule. It'd be wise of you to hurry, your first class starts at 8:30." He handed me a paper and took off down the hall.

Then I looked at the schedule he'd put together for me:

3 Hours	Physics and Theories	0830
3 Hours	A History of War and Violence	0930
3 Hours	Chemistry w/Military Applications	1330
3 Hours	Analytical Calculus	1430
10 Hours	Independent Studies w/Mentor	TBD

Ten hours a week of "independent studies" with Kain. F My Life.

{8} SLUTTY SISTER

Physics and history were lame! They aren't normal, like physics, it's not just about physics. Professor Carbonis kept referring to fieldwork, and how you could use physics based knowledge to aim a shot, set targets, and to find the perfect lookout spot. Then I went to history, and believe me, that wasn't much better. In history, Professor Smith, plain I know, said we'd be going over the modification and evolution of weapons. Oh, and did I mention there were only like three people in both of those classes.

I needed to talk to Kain, and this time he was going to give me some answers. I was on my way to the cafeteria in the Union, the main building on campus, when someone ran up behind me and put their hands over my eyes.

"Guess who? And guess fast because we have to talk!" There's only one person with a voice like that. Sadie.

"Sadie, what can we possibly have to talk about?" I couldn't stand this girl, but I figured since I'd be forced to live with her for a year, I better get used to her.

"Oh I don't know, maybe the fact that your hottie mentor brought a bag to our room and left this note," she handed me a blue sticky note, "what have you been up to Miss Carrie Lynn?"

The note said: "Babe, you left your clothes in my room when you left this morning. –K"

I am going to kill him. I think I'll strangle him, or possibly just torture him until he cries "uncle." I was never going to hear the end of this.

"Trust me Sadie, it was nothing even remotely close to what your thinking. What's your schedule like anyways?" I asked trying to change the subject. Of course, with her one-track mind, it worked.

"My classes are so fun!" Clearly we did not have the same schedule, "This morning I had Pottery and US History, and then after lunch I have Zoology, Shakespearian Literature, and Algebra. My pottery class is just full of tortured artist types that are in dying need of the comfort and company of Sadie! What classes did you get?" W.T.F.?! Why didn't she have these weird, lame, hard classes, or Independent studies? Just another reason to kill him...ugg!

"My classes are lame!" I didn't even want to try to explain them to her, so I just handed her my schedule that Dr. Beckett had given me.

"Ooo, someone gets 10 hours of hottie every week! That's gonna be so fun, especially after what happened last night. I'm glad I didn't get that though since my mentor is Evelyn. She'd probably sit there and make me be her slave. Not fun." No kidding, if this was anyone but Sadie, I'd actually feel bad for them.

"I finally met her this morning. She's a total bitch. I hope life around here gets more exciting than this." I spoke honestly. We were finally at the Union. It was the student center on campus that held all the chain fast food places that Forrestine had brought in.

"Yeah, she is. Anyways, I almost forgot the most important thing I needed to talk to you about! So I met these guys on my way to class this morning, and they invited us, well me but I don't go out alone, to their Back-to-School Bash this Friday night! They were so hot, and I call dibs on the one with black hair and green eyes. I think his name was Dylan or Daniel, something like that. But you're coming, right?" She said, she's got lungs that could compete with Michael Phelps. No normal person could say all that in one breath.

That actually did sound fun, as long as we didn't get caught, no harm, no foul.

"Sure, that sounds fun! What are you getting to eat?" I asked as I put together a salad, my usual lunch.

"I'm just getting some water and a salad. Maybe, not sure yet. Did you know we have to sit with our mentors at lunch?" A quick stop at the Starbucks barista and I was ready to check out.

"Are you serious? That is ridiculous, we're big girls, we can handle being alone for five seconds." I said as I paid for my food at the register.

I was about to be rebellious until I saw not one, but both of our mentors sitting right in front of us. Evelyn was sitting on Kain's lap while he whispered in her ear. Suddenly Evelyn turned towards us, looking at me with an evil smirk. Caught.

"Well if it isn't my newbie and the little bitch," I'm guessing the latter referred to me, "sit down, shut up, and in ten minutes, you will leave." I glared at her, but she was already back to sucking on Kain's neck. So gross! I wasn't sure why, but I had the urge to grab that nasty mess of curls she called hair, and drag her off his lap. Kain looked up and we locked eyes. Next came his trademark smirk. That was it.

I sat down and got a piece of paper out of my book bag, scribbling a quick note for Kain. Now for the fun part. I stood up, ready to test my acting skills on the fly. Hopefully it worked.

"Oh My God Kain, you promised me you wouldn't sleep with my slutty sister, I guess she forgot to tell you what the test showed," I waved the note I'd writing in their faces, "She's got three different STD's! Your disgusting, both of you! Oh, and Evelyn, you left this in the hallway." I threw the note down in front of Kain, then turned around and stormed out of the now silent cafeteria. I heard Sadie follow me, and the second we got outside we burst out laughing.

----Kain's POV----

"Oh My God Kain, you promised me you wouldn't sleep with my slutty sister, I guess she forgot to tell you what the test showed! She's got three different STD's! Your disgusting, both of you! Oh, and Evelyn, you left this in the hallway." What the fuck was she talking about? I grabbed the paper Carisma had thrown on table.

"Well isn't karma a bitch! I need to talk to you ASAP." I knew what she wanted to talk about. She wanted to know what was going on. Going to talk to her would at least give me an excuse to get away from Evelyn. She was a leech.

"I'm going to kill her. I am going to sneak into her room in the middle of the night and steal her last breath of life." I laughed at the irony of Evelyn's threat. She was a professional thief. She's been the head of some of the biggest heists that would never make it into the history books. That's how good she was, not one of her targets has ever figured out that they've been stolen from.

"Let's not forget, that's my specialty. You should really stick to your strong suits," I said pushing her off me and heading off to find Carisma.

I'd fucked Evelyn plenty of times, but that's all we were. She was convenient and, I'll admit it, I'm easy. She used to feel the same way, but lately she's been a lot clingier. It's annoying as hell. She's been hinting at me taking her on a date. Hell no. She's trying to push this into something more and I don't do relationships.

Relationships and my kind of job just don't mix. In the field, if I hesitate for one second thinking about how my imminent death would affect some girl back home, I'd be dead. Simple as that.

Morgon is crazy if he thinks this girl has any potential for this type of job. She has a family, people that love and care about her. She's not won't be able to take the type of life and death risks that I do. Unlike her, I have no one.

When I was six, my parents were murdered in our home. From what I've found, it was a shock to our town, a little suburb of Baltimore. After that, the state sent me to live with my grandmother in Holcomb, Kansas.

It was on my twelfth birthday when Morgon first approached me.

I was running through the park, we were playing hide-and-seek. I had gone really far away from the picnic table, when I ran into a man. He was a giant.

"I'm sorry," I said to him.

"It's quite alright, Kain, but I need to talk to you."

"Okay."

"I know you're not going to want to do this, but I need you to start looking into your parents death. It wasn't a home invasion."

"What? What do you mean?" He then handed me a card.

"Just call this number when you're ready." With that he turned and walked away.

Eventually, I did what he asked. I started looking into their deaths, and I got close to something. Records were being shipped to me from the Baltimore PD, but instead I arrived home to a warning. My grandmother, my only family left, had been slaughtered in her craft room. "Stop looking," was carved into the door.

That's all it took for me to call the number the Morgon had given me all those years before. The police had been in and out of the house collecting evidence, while I sat on the porch waiting for Morgon.

He brought me to the academy that night. I was sixteen, and now two years later, I was his prodigy. We both knew the only reason I had agreed to come here. I would kill them, and every job brought me one step closer.

I finally came out of my thoughts and realized I was at the dorm. Carisma was probably in her room. She had a couple hours before her next class. I went upstairs and sure enough, her and the blonde were just about to walk into their room. They were laughing; most likely from that little stunt she'd pulled at the Union.

I had to admit, I thought it was great, but I couldn't let her get away with stuff like that.

"Carisma." I said narrowing my gaze on her. She was hot, and she knew it. From the tights that flaunted her perfect ass, to the shirt that hugged her curves making me want to lock her away in my room forever. I couldn't overlook the fact that she wore such dark colors. I'd seen girls that dressed like her; they referred to themselves as 'scene.' They all seemed to be depressed or suicidal, hopefully that wasn't Carisma.

She'd want me eventually, and I could wait until she was begging for me. Evelyn would keep me entertained until then.

"Oh my cheating lover, what ever do you need?" Did she think this was a joke?

"Let's go, now!" I walked towards her, and made sure I sounded pissed, even though I wanted to congratulate here for the look she left on Evelyn's face as she stormed out.

"No," she said glaring at me. I could swear there was almost pure hate in her eyes.

I grabbed her arm and started pulling her towards my room. My room was awesome; it was like a small apartment. I think Morgon was trying to make up for the fact that I had nowhere to go. I lived here year round.

"RAPE, RAPE, RAPE! HELP HE'S KIDNAPPING ME!" I clamped a hand over her mouth.

"Shut the hell up, you said we needed to talk. So talk. I can't give you all the answers you want, but I can give you some of them." I told her once we were in my apartment. Morgon had made it clear that I was not to tell her what her specialty was going to be yet.

She looked confused. I probably shocked her by being nice, or at least as close to nice as I got. She sat down on my couch, then the questions started flying out.

"What is this school? Why don't I have the same classes as everyone else? Why do I have ten hours of training with you? Who decided to switch my mentors and why? What's wrong with Mason, why does he think he's not fit for duty?" She finally took a breath. New plan.

"Okay maybe this would be easier if I just told you what I can, then you can ask questions."

"I guess" She looked nervous about this. I knew what that was like, you wanted the truth, and then you got it. And more often than not, it was pretty damn ugly.

"The Elite Academy is a early-entry to college program for most students that come here. For a very select few, maybe one every three years, it is something more. We train free agents, and we only train the best. Morgon seems to think you would be the perfect fit for our little group." Here she interrupted me.

"What's a free agent?" This was going to be difficult to explain. What the hell, Morgon can deal with the consequences of trying to make Scene Barbie here an assassin.

"A free agent is many things, however we typically specialize in one field. It could be infiltration, collection, or cleaning. An infiltration agent gathers information, that would be Mason. Collection means taking things that aren't yours to be taking, stealing to be blunt, and that would be Evelyn. A cleaner makes people disappear. That's me." I expected her to look at me like I was crazy, but instead she looked like everything finally made sense to her.

"What does any of that have to do with me?" Her voice was shaking, and she looked worried. Damn, maybe I should've listened to Morgon.

----Carrie's POV----

"The Elite Academy is a early-entry to college program for most students that come here. For a very select few, maybe one every three years, it is something more. We train free agents, and we only train the best. Morgon seems to think you would be the perfect fit for our little group." Kain wasn't answering any of my questions; in fact, I could feel new ones piecing themselves together in my mind. I settled with asked the most relevant question at the moment.

"What's a free agent?" He thought for a few seconds, it looked like he was arguing back and forth in his head whether or not to answer me. I was getting annoyed by his pacing back and forth, in front of my on the couch. Surprisingly, it was quite comfortable. It was black leather, and across from it was a simple black coffee table. While the apartment fit him, it just seemed somehow staged. There was nothing personal anywhere unless you count the magazines neatly placed on the table.

"A free agent is many things, however we typically specialize in one field. It could be infiltration, collection, or cleaning. An infiltration agent gathers information, that would be Mason. Collection means taking things that aren't yours to be taking, stealing to be blunt, and that would be Evelyn. A cleaner makes people disappear. That's me." A cleaner. What did that mean? Did he hide people? Kidnap them? God forbid, kill them? If he is a cleaner, and he is training me, that means Morgon expects me to also become a cleaner.

Oh my god. I could feel my throat start to tighten as my breathing became more rapid. I was going to hyperventilate, and present company would probably let me. I had to stop thinking like that or I was never going to get my breathing back to normal. I needed to ask questions. That's the only way I was going to get the twisting knot in my stomach to go away.

"What does any of that have to do with me?" I finally choked out. I held on to the couch with a white-knuckle grip anticipating his answer.

He had stopped pacing for a few minutes and was just staring at me. I knew he heard me.

"Damnit, Kain, what does that mean? You're my mentor, does that mean I'm supposed to be a cleaner?" I was kicking myself for ever having wanted these answers. It was too much, way too fast. Oh, and to make it all better, even after my outburst, he still wasn't answering me.

Fine, I'd use a different approach. I made my way around the table and stood in front of him so there was no way he could ignore me. I knew what happened to me whenever we touched, and I figured if he experienced anything like that, it would be just enough of a distraction to get through the wall he'd put up. He had his hands in his pockets, so I gently grabbed his wrists and pulled them out, and then slid my hands down and laced my fingers with his.

"Please, Kain. What you're not telling me is scaring the hell out of me." I would be lying if I said I wasn't really scared, but I was definitely exaggerating the extent of it. I stepped forward, getting as close to him as possible, searching his eyes for any hint of defeat.

"I don't know why Morgon thinks you'd, in his words, make the perfect partner for me. He doesn't want me out in the field alone anymore, says I'm getting reckless. Normal people shouldn't have to do what I do. You shouldn't do what I do. I kill people." I could feel his warm breath as he spoke every word. It distracted me so it took me a few seconds to register what he had said, especially the last thing.

He kills people. He doesn't show it in his face, but I can tell by his voice that he feels guilty about that statement. I should be disgusted with him, maybe even hate him, but I couldn't.

Morgon wants me to kill people. Well, maybe not pull the trigger, but to help Kain pull the trigger. I felt a shiver go through my body. I wanted to help him. Not help him kill people, but there had to be a reason he started doing this.

"Why? What made you take this job?" I said at barely a whisper.

I was surprised when he actually answered my question, but I wasn't expecting what he said. He told me about his parents being killed, being sent to Kansas with his Grandmother, looking into his parents death, and finally the warning. He'd been through so much in his eighteen years. We were still standing together in the middle of the living room, and he didn't notice when a tear slid down his cheek.

I wasn't sure why, but I had the urge to kiss him, to finally feel his lips on mine. I leaned up, expecting for him to reject me, but he didn't. He met me halfway, crashing his lips on mine with an urgency I could match. I needed more. I slid my hands up his solid chest and around his neck. Tangling my fingers in his silky hair, I pulled him into me, making him moan into my mouth. His tongue glided over my bottom lip, asking for entrance, which I happily granted. We stayed that way for a while, just exploring each other with our tongues. When we finally broke apart, we were breathing hard. I hadn't noticed when he'd wrapped his arms around my waist, but it felt right. I didn't regret anything that we'd just done; I looked up hoping that he agreed.

"Yes." That's the only word that made sense about anything. I knew what he wanted was revenge, that's why he took this job. He didn't have to say it. Everything in me was telling me to help him, to protect him, to save him. That's what I wanted to do, even though he probably didn't think he needed it, and it scared me to death. I was ready.

"What do you mean?" He face actually showed emotions for once. It was a combination of scared, confused, and unsure.

I kissed him gently once more, and he responded. I could feel butterflies in my stomach, and I knew if I didn't stop this kiss soon, I'd forget the rest of what I was trying to say, so I pulled away from him.

"Yes, I will. I will be your partner. I will put up with your hellish training sessions, and I will become the best."

He was searching my eyes, trying to find any glimmer of doubt, but there wasn't any to find.

"Do you know what that means? You'll do what I do." I knew I was about to agree to go against everything I'd been taught, but I there was a reason I was put here. Once again, the only word that fit:

"Yes."

{11} COLD FLOATING CLOUDS

I stopped complaining about my training sessions with Kain. God, so much had happened and it has only been two days. Our training hours the next three days were spent with Kain judging my skill level in various areas of physical aptitude, as he put it. Tuesday was spent running continuous sprints for two hours while dodging a paint ball gun. The paint ball gun was meant to increase my awareness and better my dodging technique. As far as I'm concerned it only gave me pastel colored bruises. Wednesday I was actually excited when I found out we were meeting at the pool. Wrong. Treading water for two hours is not as easy as it sounds. Especially when your wearing a sweatpants and shirt.

Nothing really exciting happened in my classes, but really, how could it. I'm practically the only student in them! I was sitting in analytical calculus, isn't that fun to say, staring out the window. Today, has been the only nice, mildly hot, yet pleasant day and I'm stuck inside. Awesome. This was by far my biggest class with a whopping twelve students! Ugg, today we were learning about some rule, I should probably listen, but I just really wasn't into it today.

I was anxious to get to the gym where I was meeting Kain for our training session. All I had to do was run, granted it was on a treadmill which was kind of lame, but still, Kain was just monitoring how my heart and lungs reacted after certain stages of exhaustion. He said that in order to be field-cleared I had to be able to physically handle the strain of running until I'm exhausted, then running some more. Ha, he got stuck with the boring job of watching the screens full of graphs that meant nothing to me. Since whatever it was happened between us, he's been a lot more forthcoming about the exercises we are doing, and explaining it's purpose.

I didn't even notice that everyone was getting up to leave the room until I felt someone tap me on the shoulder. After a little jump, I looked up to see Mason standing over me. Weird, What was he doing here?

"What's so fascinating?" His eyes were still that haunting blue-grey. I don't think they are naturally that color, something happened, on a job probably.

"It's a beautiful day outside and I really just want to go out and lay in the grass. Can't you hear it calling me?" I laughed, showing him I was joking... not crazy.

"Then why don't you? I can see a spot from here that looks perfect. We can work on this huge assignment Mr. Bovey gave us." Oh monkey tails, maybe I should have paid attention. Oh well, too late now anyways.

"I can't, I've got training with Kain," I looked at my watch, "in five minutes! I've got to go. Bye Mason! Do you happen to be going to the back-to-school party tomorrow night?" I flashed my million-dollar smile. It was like good luck; with it I always got my way.

"Yeah I am actually, I guess I'll see you there?" He was staring at my lips, but sadly, that only made me think of Kain, and the kiss we'd shared. I smashed my eyes shut to try to get the memory to go away. We hadn't even talked about it since then. I'm not sure if this is a good thing or a bad thing.

"Of course! Well I have to get to the gym before Kain murders me. See you later!" I said as I turned and rushed out the door, running for the gym. Luckily I had thrown my running clothes in my book bag this morning, so there's the slight chance that I won't be late.

The gym was on the very top floor of our dorm, I'm not sure why, but hey, whatever works. I decided to take the elevator so that I'd be able to change.

Stepping on, I noticed the security camera in the corner. I took my jacket off and tied it over the camera. I got changed into my favorite pink sports bra and lime green soffe shorts. It's a good thing the elevator didn't stop on any other floors before I got up here. I got my jacket off the camera and put it on over my sports bra and zipped it up, just in case any pervs got on between here and the gym.

I was just finishing stuffing my jeans in my bag when the elevator dinged and opened, revealing a pissed looking Kain.

"Your late." That's all he said, but he didn't use his scary voice, which I thought was strange. He seemed to like trying to scare me into submission, just because he knew eventually he could. Maybe this was just a new approach.

"Sorry, I spaced out during class and I'd still be sitting there if Mason hadn't of woken me up." I looked at him and saw what could be mistaken as jealousy in his eyes, but it was gone just as soon as it appeared.

"No big deal, I just need to get the heart monitor leads put on you, then you'll be ready to run. " Whoa, I was expecting screaming and yelling. I wasn't going to complain that's for sure. I took off my jacket, and let Kain put the little sticky things on me. He looked down my body and I felt the temperature rise. I tried to ignore it and started running on the treadmill.

The run was so boring! Kain took my iPod from me; apparently, when you're outrunning terrorists and drug dealers, they don't let you have a 20 second head start to strap your iPod to your arm. Lame! I resorted to singing my favorite songs in my head, and before I knew it I was done.

I collapsed on the floor, just laid down, it's not like I was in anyone's way. Kain had the gym cleared out for the evening so there wouldn't be any distractions.

"That was amazing. Your lung capacity grew, while your heart rate lowered and then leveled out. Runners normally have lower heart rates, but usually it speeds up before it slows down." I hadn't noticed he had moved until he spoke. He was standing over me with one foot on each side of my waist.

"So did I pass whatever field test this was?" I was overheating, although I wasn't sure what the cause was, my workout or my mentor. I grabbed my water bottle, and drizzled some water on my face. Oh my gosh, something never felt so amazing.

"Well this was supposed to be me seeing what we needed to work on, but with stats like that, I don't have anything to work on for endurance." Thank the lord, if I had to train like this often, I'd die.

"Sweet, so what are we doing tomorrow?" I asked him, still lying on the amazingly comfortable hard gym floor.

"Actually, we aren't doing anything tomorrow. I have a job and I'm leaving tonight," He glanced at his watch, "in forty five minutes to be exact. Come on let's get out of here."

"Okay, that's perfect! I need to go get a spray tan I guess. I haven't been able to spend anytime outside, people should just start calling me Casper." It was true, I didn't normally sound like a vain plastic Barbie doll, but I'd never had to worry about being tan because I spent enough time outside.

I had the party with Sadie tomorrow night and I had found the perfect dress in the back of my closet. It was a tight, strapless dress that went to my mid thigh. It had slits up each side that went up the my hip and were laced together with a thick white ribbon, so it wasn't like you could actually see all the way up to my hip.

"Where are you going tomorrow night?" I wasn't sure I wanted to tell him what I was doing.

"Where are you going tonight?" I countered, trying to change the subject.

"That's classified information as far as your concerned."

"I thought Morgon didn't want you to go out alone anymore." Success, subject changed.

"He doesn't, but he can't ignore the money that my skills bring in." By this time we had arrived at my door.

"Well then I guess I'll see you when you get back?" I was hinting at him telling me when he'd get back.

"Yeah, we'll start strength training Monday. Be ready." He said turning away, off to his room to pack for a mysterious destination.

I went and took a shower. I was exhausted, so after my shower I decided just to crash for the night. When I got back to my room, I put on my pajamas and was about to lose myself under the covers of my bed when I noticed a paper sitting on my pillow with a key taped to it.

"Carisma-

Just in case you need it.

-K"

Strange, but I went ahead and put the key on my keychain with all the rest. It was definitely time to sleep. I felt like I was going to pass out.

|||||||||||||| FRIDAY NIGHT ||||||||||||||

I had just got back from getting my tan. I wasn't anywhere near as dark as I'd normally be, but I didn't want to look orange. I settled with a few shades darker than Casper. I put on my dress, which was looking pretty hot if I do say so myself. With it, I wore a pair of cute white Gucci Iman Platforms that I borrowed from Sadie, and white hoop earrings.

Sadie looked like the playboy version of a schoolgirl, but should I really have expected anything different. We grabbed our bags and made a dash for the party. It started an hour ago, but everyone knows that aparty doesn't really start for another hour or two. According to Sadie, these guys house was just off campus, so we were walking.

There were red cups everywhere, and the place smelled like a brewery, but everyone seemed to be having fun, which is what I needed today. I decided I'd drink water for a while until I finished debating what I wanted to drink, if I wanted to drink. I found out that there wasn't any music because they were still waiting for the DJ. Lame. Sadie and I wandered around making up a rating system for the guys at the party.

Finally, the DJ got there and with music coursing through our veins, the party really started. I ran into Mason at the bar when I'd finally decided to have a drink.

"Are you having fun?" He yelled over the music and flashed a smile that almost made him seem generally happy.

"Definitely," I screamed, "Straight vodka shot." I told the bartender when he finally showed up.

"What kind of vodka?" the slimly looking bartender asked, clearly ignoring the fact that I wasn't anywhere near twenty-one.

"Absolut," I told him then turned back to Mason

"Seriously, straight vodka? That's pretty hard." He looked a little concerned.

"Oh yes, all or nothing baby," I said downing the shot, signaling for another.

"I guess, just don't kill yourself Carrie." He joked.

"I won't," I slammed the glass on the counter and grabbed Mason's hand, "Let's dance."

He smiled and followed me to the dance floor. OMG by Usher was playing, the perfect club dancing song. I wrapped my hands around Mason's neck and he put his hands on my waist, moving to the music. I turned around and started grinding my butt on him.

"Mmm You're really sexy you know." Mason whispered into my ear making me smile. We kept dancing until the song ended, then went back to the bar for more drinks.

I had just finished my fifth shot when I felt someone tap me on the shoulder. Yeah, I know shots are bad, especially five at my size, but I needed to lose myself, just for the night. I turned around to see none other than my favorite person ever, Evelyn Rooks.

"May I help you with something favorite sister ever!?" I asked referring to the cafeteria incident.

"What exactly do you think your doing with Mason?" I looked around not seeing him anywhere, weird; I could have sworn he was right beside me at the bar.

"Well I was having a hell of a lot of fun until you showed up."

61

"Stay away from him you little slut." That was the last straw. I slapped her across the face.

"Did you really just do that?" She laughed in response. Never mind, her actual response was the fist that just slammed into my cheek. I touched my cheek where she'd hit and felt the warm sticky blood starting to inch it's way down my face.

I pulled my arm back and aimed for the perfect spot on her cute little face. Throwing all I could into the punch, I hit her in the nose. I better have freaking broke it was all I could think as I took off to the dorm. I was about to unlock Sadie and my door when I thought about the screaming she was going to do when she got back for punching her mentor. I saw the extra key hanging off my chain and I knew where to go.

I kept walking down the hallway to Kain's door and let myself in using the key he'd left me. I slipped my shoes off and lay down on couch for a while, only intending to stay long enough for Sadie to get home and pass out.

Tomorrow was going to be awesome. Evelyn would no doubt tell Morgon that I'd broken her pretty little face, and he'd have Kain put me through some horrible workout for the next month. It was too much to think about, and eventually I just fell asleep.

I was having weird dreams all night. I felt cold and hot at the same time, and then I felt like I was floating and landed on a cloud in heaven. I've definitely had too much to drink.

----Kain's POV----

This was the part of the job I hated. The long ass plane rides. Today, I was headed to somewhere in Cambodia. I was in the Academy's jet, which, according to government records, doesn't exist. I guess a long time ago an agent did a favor for the president. The job came with significant perks; the Academy and the agents that work for it don't even pay taxes.

Since this was the Academy's jet, there weren't even any flirty flight attendants to entertain me. Nope, just me, Fred the pilot and Charlie the copilot. The worst thing about flights like this is that it leaves me time to think. I do not want to think. It will lead to me thinking about what happened Monday.

God, I hadn't meant to tell her anything about me. That was kind of my trademark, no one but Morgon knew my history. Not even Evelyn. I just felt the words come and I had no will to stop them. I sat down in one of the royal blue airline quality seats and relaxed. Not too much of course, that was impossible. You'd think they could at least get some nice, first-class seats.

Great now I sound like a whiney little brat. I couldn't stop thinking about that night. Well day I guess, but whatever, it seemed to last forever. Afterwards, Carisma just said yes. I stared at her for the longest time, waiting, searching for doubt, regret, even lies. But there was none, she had put every bit of truth into that one word.

She backed it up too. She hasn't complained once about our training session, even started showing up on time. Mostly. Yeah, I've been pushing her extra hard the past few days, just because I could. I was waiting for her to break and change her mind, but she hasn't. Something is telling me that she won't.

I'm acting like such a girl thinking about this shit. Oh well, at least no one else knows I'm doing it. If this were any other girl, I'd talk to Mason about it. But that wasn't really possible since the accident. He was just sort of vacant from reality. I wish I knew what had went down in France, but Morgon wasn't telling anybody and I wasn't about to risk asking Mason or Evelyn about it. I don't even know if Evelyn knows, but she was there.

"We will be arriving in Cambodia in fifteen minutes, Mr. Tandem. Sir Morgon has your usual car waiting on the strip, he says it is stocked with all the supplies you requested at Quantico." The copilot said. I never asked why Charlie called Morgon "Sir," but whatever works I guess.

"Thanks Charlie" I responded. I couldn't wait to get behind the wheel of my car. I actually had two of them, one for the job, and one for my personal use. Aston Martin V12 Vanquish Carbon Black Limited Edition.

This job was a special under the table request from Quantico, which really meant it was from US Department of Defense. Our wonderful Secretary of Defense Andrew Wellington, the head of the DOD, was failing at his current goal that was to establish a communication with Cambodian drug lord and human trafficker Raphael Euphoric. They say his drugs induce euphoria. Maybe that's how he acquired his last name.

Euphoric was preventing the implementation of a defensive policy that has been in the works between the US and Cambodia for ages. At least that's what I got from what they told me at the Quantico briefing. I felt the plane begin to shake as we started our descent. God, all this damn technology and we can't get rid of turbulence. What the hell?

"We're here Mr. Tandem. Good luck and thank you for flying with Elite Airways today." I laughed at Fred's announcement. Like I had a choice. Once we had landed, the door flipped open forming the good old-fashioned stairway down to the landing strip.

"Thanks Fred, Charlie, I'll be seeing you soon." I said waving at them as I walked off. As promised, there was my baby. I didn't plan on this job taking long, I really just wanted to get a good weekend long sleep in. It was Friday afternoon, so if I got the job done quick, which I could, I'd get home by eleven tonight. Awesome.

I slipped into the car's custom leather interior as I flipped through the folder of information I'd been given about Euphoric. Apparently they'd already sent two of their "professional" assassins, but they were killed by Euphoric before they even got their scope out. Psh, so that's why they called me in. They can't risk losing anymore of the US's snipers to a drug lord that they are supposed to be negotiating with, not killing.

Normally I hated this job. The guilt was almost unbearable, but I didn't let anyone else know that. I wasn't born a killer. As I stared down at the photo I'd been given of Raphael Euphoric, I knew this one wouldn't be anything more than a slight breeze on the conscience of this killer. In the photo, he was holding a gun to a young girl's head. She was maybe six, eight at the most. The caption said it was his own daughter. He used her as a shield during an attempted police invasion of one of his homes. When he was far enough from the police to get away in his car, he "eliminated" his own daughter.

Nope, I would sleep easy after this job. I was about to do the world a huge favor. I followed the horrendous directions until I was heading up a hill that supposedly overlooked Euphoric's main compound. I cut the lights during my ascent, the last thing I needed was to be given away because of the headlights. At the top of the hill, I turned the car so it was ready to fly down the hill within seconds, and parked.

The best thing about this car was the quiet engine and acceleration. I'd be down this hill and halfway back to the jet before they realized what had happened. I hit the small button conveniently hidden under the gas pedal, which made the custom back seat lift, revealing my precious weapons.

I grabbed my M24 Sniper Weapon System and the Smith & Wesson 22 caliber. I also grabbed the silencer and secured it to the revolver. I was ready. I set up the M24, looking down over Eurphoric's swimming pool. I had the 22 laid under my chest, just in case I needed it up here.

I had been on this hellfire hot hill for at least two hours when Euphoric finally came out side and lay down on a pool chair. He looked like he was tanning, what a freak. I remember Carrie saying something about tanning; she was probably doing that right now. Damnit, this was the kind of distraction I needed to avoid. It was time to get this job over with and get home. I leveled the crosshairs on his head. I pulled the trigger and shut my eyes; I hated seeing the look of them as they died. It didn't last long of course, but still; it would just be more to think about later.

I shot him once more in the heart. Another one of my trademarks, two shots. Head and Heart, no survivors. I had gathered the guns and packed them away, time to return to the strip. On my way back I called Morgon.

"Springtime Manor Pennsylva-"

"Ignis," I said the code word, interrupting the pre-recorded answering machine. I waited for it to redirect me to Morgon.

"Tandem, so soon, this is good news I hope."

"Yes sir, target down. I'm heading back to the jet now."

"Well, I sure expected it to take longer than four hours."

"Yeah, so did I, but the target decided it was a good day for tanning."

"Very well, Fred and Charlie have been notified, and are ready on the tarmac. Leave the Vanquish where you found it and we'll get it back to the garage."

"Sounds good boss, I meet you at the office tomorrow for all the official crap."

"You know not to call me boss, Tandem. I'll have everything ready by one and Quantico just got word of a drug lord being taken out in a turf war down in Cambodia. Your payment is being wired now. I'll talk to you tomorrow."

"You know not to call me Tandem, boss, you're like my second dad. Anyways, I'll see you tomorrow." I said hanging up. I had arrived at the jet, placing the folder on Euphoric under the seat, where one of the garage guys would remove and destroy it forever.

I was exhausted; I collapsed into one of the seats on the jet and fell into a deep sleep. Before I knew it, I had fallen into a deep, dreamless slumber. But, as usual, it didn't last long.

I woke up as I fell off the seats I had made into a makeshift bed. Damn turbulence. That must mean we're arriving at the Academy. Thank god.

"We have arrived at the Academy, thank you for flying with Elite Airlines." Charlie's signature sign off echoed through the cabin.

"Only the best." I said leaning into the cockpit. "As always, thank you guys. I'll see you next time."

"Your welcome, Mr. Tandem. We'll be seeing you later than." Fred said opening the door and releasing me from the flying box of death.

Luckily the landing spot was right on top of Marshall hall. I punched in the code on the roof access door and made my way down to my floor. The closer I got the longer it seemed to take to get there. Just as I was about to unlock my door, when I felt arms snake around my waist. I so did not want to deal with this tonight.

"What do you want Evelyn?" I asked in the most polite voice I could manage.

"I want you to make that little bitch pay. Make her hurt so bad she wants to give up, then let me at her." What was she talking about?

I turned around and barely caught my laughter at the site of Evelyn. Clearly her nose had been broken, and since she wanted at Carrie, I'm guessing she's the one that did this.

"So let me get this straight, you want me to push her until she's exhausted, and then let you go at her. That's probably the only way you could kick her ass, what did you do to her?" I watched as Evelyn's eyes shifted to the floor. This wasn't going to be good.

"I may have called her a slut, but she deserved it. She's dressed like a playboy bunny, and was grinding all over every guy in sight." I felt my fists clench when she mentioned Carrie grinding all over guys.

"Well I'm sorry, but you deserved what you got. Now, if you don't mind, I'm going to sleep," I saw her smirk and start to say something, "alone." I made clear.

"Whatever." She said making her way back down the hall to her room.

I unlocked my door, relaxing into my nice cool air-conditioned sanctuary. I shut the door and threw my shoes off, when I heard a sigh. I turned on instinct prepared to fight, when I saw her. She was asleep on my couch. I relaxed and walked closer to her, there was a pretty deep gash on her cheek. I'm guessing that's what led to Evelyn's broken nose. I went to the kitchen and got a wet washcloth to clean off the blood, she was going to need stitches, but they could wait till morning.

As I wiped the blood off her cheek, she shifted and murmured something about the cold. I was finished with the blood and leaving the washcloth on the table, I picked her up. She looked amazing in the short black dress, nothing like the playboy slut Evelyn tried to make her out to be.

I laid her in my bed and saw her smile as she relaxed into the black down comforter. My room was basic, black and white. As with most of the apartment, there were no personal items left out, and most of my cabinets were locked. I had weapons almost everywhere. I stripped down to my boxers, my usual sleeping attire and climbed into my side of the bed.

Hopefully there would be no nightmares in my sleep tonight. It had been awhile since I had actually gotten a full night of sleep. With the look in her eyes that day, I think she just might be the angel that saves me from hell. With that thought, I fell into the most peaceful sleep since I'd arrived at the academy.

----Carrie's POV----

I don't remember my bed being this comfortable. There is no way I'm getting up early today, especially not with this persistent pounding in my head. Last night was definitely not one of my better ideas. The last this I remember was knocking back shots at the bar with Mason. I opened my eyes up, but just a slit to avoid the shearing pain that was bound to happen. Surprisingly, the room I was in was pitch black. I couldn't see anything. I was not in my room. Oh god, please tell me I did not go home with Mason.

Ripping the blankets off, I saw that I was still in my dress from the party, which was a good thing, minus the fact that what seemed hot and sexy last night, now felt like a vacuum-sealed saran wrapped prison. I'm not really sure how that would work exactly, but points for trying right. So, I'm not in my room and I clearly didn't have sex with anyone. I did not plan to be one of those horrible statistics that lost their virginity and could even remember the guy's name, then three weeks later you find out your pregnant and it's ju... what the heck? I ramble a lot.

Just as I was debated possible escapes from wherever I was, I heard a door creak open, and heard footsteps approaching the bed. Scrambling to the middle of the bed, I thought of the likeliness that I would be able to find a weapon from this position and in this lighting that I was so thankful for not even three minutes ago, I knew it would be impossible.

"I'm afraid at this point, you would be as good as dead." Kain's voice echoed through the darkness. I couldn't decide whether it was a good or a bad thing that it was him that seemed to have found me in this state.

"What are you doing here?" I asked pulling the blanket up around myself. I'm not sure why, but suddenly I felt like such an exposed slut. Bad, it was definitely bad that it was Kain. He turned on a light by the bed, causing the dull pounding the previously graced my head to become a freight train bouncing back and fourth as if it were a bumper car.

"Well, seeing as this is my apartment, the better question would be what are you doing here?" I opened my mouth to come up with some lame excuse on the fly, but he put his hand up signaling for me to stop. " But, I think I got most of the explanation from Evelyn's face. She got you good, but I'm proud to say it appears you came back at her with a hundred times the force. Not that I'm condoning violence against your peers, its just more proof that I am truly amazing." Wow someone had an ego this morning.

"Ha, I could throw a perfectly good punch before I ever met you, so don't go taking too much credit for that."

"Whatever. I need to put a couple stitches in that gash on your cheek, or your going to have one nasty scar. We have a meeting with the committee in a couple hours. There's coffee on the dresser, bathroom is to the left and your clothes are on the counter, that is unless you would like to wear what you have on."

"What committee? Did you sleep with me?" I asked just now noticing that there was clearly more than one occupant in this bed last night. And what the hell was the committee?

"You'll meet the committee soon enough and trust me, you'll wish you hadn't. Now I'll need you to be ready by 1230, I will be escorting you to the meeting as your mentor. And yes, I did sleep in my bed, which I was nice enough to share with the girl who smelled like she went for a swim in the Absolut brewery." He emphasized the fact that it was his bed. Psh, whatever.

Knowing it would give him way to much pleasure to see the pain that this hangover was putting me through, I jumped up and grabbed the coffee and took off to the bathroom with an energy similar to that of a sugar-filled 5-year-old.

I stood in the shower and let the water wash over me. I loved water, I remember once telling my mother I wanted to be a mermaid, and I always hated Ariel because she had my dream life. I felt like the water was taking away not only the dirt and grime I felt like I was covered in, but also the pain left over from the hangover. The water also betrayed me, like little piercing daggers to the gash Kain had indicated on my cheek. He wasn't lying when he said I'd be scarred without stitches, heck I'd probably be scarred with them, but I guess it's worth a shot.

Stepping out of the shower, I wrapped myself in the black towel that was sitting on a shelf by the shower door, and took a look at the clothes I'd be wearing to this daunting committee meeting. I knew I just have to deal with them, since I wouldn't have time to go to my room and get ready and get back here to get stitches. Plus it'd probably look bad to make the dash from Kain's apartment to my room in only a towel. Sadie would really have a story for the masses then.

There was a black high-wasted skirt that came to about five inches above my knee, a white tank top and button-up blouse, and a rather cute cropped black blazer to top it off. On a more disturbing note, also on the counter was a bra and underwear that still had the Victoria's Secret tag on them. While I'll admit they were pretty cute and fit just right, I didn't want to know how Kain had picked them out so well. Sitting by the door were a pair of heels, four inches and plain black. I slipped them on and took in the image in the mirror on the back of the door, definitely looking like a secretary. I didn't like that fact at all, but it could be worse.

Grabbing the coffee mug that I'd left on the counter, I sipped it while I waited for my hair to semi dry so I could do something with it, I'm pretty sure blow-drying and straightening aren't going to be an option. When I finished my coffee, I gave my hair a quick fluff and hoped it would look halfway decent by the time this meeting came around. Leaving the bathroom, I realized I didn't know which door in the bedroom led to the living room. This was so lame. Why couldn't we all have nice little apartments? I'd be perfectly content with living with Sadie if we had this much space.

After walking into not one, but two different closets, I finally found the right door. Why did a guy like Kain need so many closets? He was waiting on the couch, looking through a file that must belong to one of his top-secret-disappear-off-the-map-for-a-few-days-and-kill-someone cases. I stood in front of him with my hand on my hips, waiting to get this stitch crap over with. I hate needles. He looked me up and down, which bothered me a little.

"Well, stitches sometime today?" I asked when he wasn't moving from his spot on the massive black leather beast of a couch.

"Someone's anxious to get sewn up like a ragdoll." A shiver passed through me and I heard him laugh, knowing he could tell I was going to hate every bit of this needle stuff.

I followed him to the kitchen and hopped up on the counter, waiting for him to get this needle ready. Sitting on countertops was an annoying habit I'd had for as long as I remember, one that my mother hated, but eventually gave up on making me stop. He turned around and stood in front of me, we were about at eye level, which was definitely a plus considering he was about to come at my face with a giant, hot, pointy, sharp needle.

"This will probably work best if you look up at the ceiling. And, I need to be able to get a little closer to your face." He said, with a smirk I'm sure, as I looked down and realized the only way to make that work was going to end up very awkward. I scooted up to the very edge of the counter and he moved so that I had one leg on each side of him. Anyone that walked in right now would get a very wrong idea of what was going on.

"Ugg, can we just get this over with please? I hate needles." I complained looked intently at the ceiling fan above us.

I felt the needle as it entered my face and willed myself to stay as still as stone. Even though everything inside me was threatening to scream bloody murder. But before I had a chance to, Kain's voice broke my concentration.

"All done, come on, we have to get to the committee." He said, gripping my waist and placing me gently on the floor.

"What is the committee and why are we meeting with them?" I hoped he would, for once, just give me a straight answer.

"They are sort of like the check-and-balancing system at Elite, and they are here today to approve or deny Morgon's latest decision. You." This did not sound good.

"Do I have to talk to them?" I asked Kain as we approached the all too familiar door of Headmaster Morgon.

"Only if they ask something of you. Also, out of respect, assume the position. Feet shoulder width apart, hands resting on your lower back and eyes straight ahead." He had his this-is-business voice on, and got finished just as the heavy oak door swung open revealing the vast open space that was supposedly an office.

Once again I found myself walking across the hall towards the Headmaster. Today, his ornate desk had been replaced by a half-circle table which was surrounded by three men, one being Headmaster Morgon. I didn't know the one on the right, but the other one looked familiar. He didn't look that old at all, maybe 24 at the most.

"Gentlemen, I'd like to introduce you to the newest member of our team, Carisma Larson. This meeting was not supposed to take place for a few more weeks, but I'm afraid it had to be moved up due to some unforeseen events." Headmaster Morgon had stood to introduce me, and now took his seat. I wonder what the "unforeseen events" were.

"Mr. Tandem, please report to the committee on the progress of Ms. Larson." What progress? I'd only been here like a week. What the heck?

"Well, seeing as how we've only had Ms. Larson with us for a week, there hasn't been much time to see any progress. However, her foundation skills are excellent. The numbers from her cardio test are amazing, they almost compete with mine and I've been training for two years. Endurance is adequate, and she's almost field ready from the start. At least as back up. I wouldn't place her in a mission on her own yet, but she's good. The only problem I've noted is her apparent disregard for authority, which mostly took place in the first two days I worked with her." Is he serious? I am going to kick his ass! I do not disregard authority; I disregarded his stupid, pushy, jerk-ness. I was fighting my hardest not to move an inch while he was saying this.

"However, I would feel confident in saying that it was due to Agent Bethesda being pulled off her case and being replaced with myself without explanation. We all know that I am not the easiest to get along with." He continued.

"So am I to understand correctly that you are taking complete responsibility for her obstinate behavior, Agent Tandem?" The man on the right had spoken.

"Yes sir." Hmm I'm not sure yet it this makes up for what he said earlier, but maybe I won't attack him later. Just yell.

"Well then, I guess its time for the official approvals. I, Steel Morgon, approve." Next was the man to the right.

"I, Grant Tiers, approve." Next was the man on the left.

"I, Tanner Larson, do not approve." What? When he said this, I chanced looking down. Headmaster Morgon and Grant Tiers, the man on the right, had turned to look at the third man. Apparently they were as confused as I was. Headmaster Morgon cleared his throat and turned back to face Kain and myself. I snapped my head back up to looking at the wall across from me.

"Well, with two-thirds majority, Carisma Larson, welcome to the Elite. I'd like to see you both in my office Monday, now if you'll please excuse us."

I was ready to get out of there. I'm not sure why but it was really way too intense for my liking. It was a weird coincidence that the third guy had the same last name as me. My dad didn't have any brothers or sisters. I had heard the whispers start when we were a little over halfway to the door.

"No! You are not sending my sister out there! And especially not with him!" I stopped dead in my tracks. What, his sister? I didn't have any siblings. I was about to turn around when I felt a hand on my arm. Kain was dragging me out of the room. Oh, now he is really going to get it. The doors to the room slammed shut behind us.

"What do you think your doing?" I started yelling at Kain, clawing at his arm, trying to get him off me.

"Carisma, stop." Great now he had both my wrists. He led me into the stairwell before saying anything else.

"Let go of me Kain." I demanded.

"No, you can't go back in there."

"Why not? You heard what he said, what's he talking about?" I was about to go all ninja on him and kick him where the sun doesn't shine. It's like he knew what I was thinking because next thing I know he has me slammed up against the wall. Again. To think, just a few days ago, we were in this exact position on much different circumstances.

"I heard what he said. But even if I let you go, you'd never get past those doors. Now, when I let go please just come with me. I'm not asking you to ignore that, just to think stuff through a little." I could feel his hot breath tickling my cheek as he spoke. He sounded different, almost pleading for me to make this easy for him. He was right, what was I going to do? I guess I could call my parents.

But if they lied to me for this long, I'd imagine they could withstand lying over the phone.

"Fine. Let's go." I didn't mean to be such a B to him; out of everyone here he's probably been the nicest.

We walked in silence, I was lost in thought, and he was just letting me go with it. I'm so confused. I need to get my phone from his apartment, and then I'm going to call my parents. It's worth a shot right.

"Are you coming in?"

"Huh," I looked around, I didn't notice we were already in the dorm, "oh, yeah."

I walked in and grabbed my cell phone that was laying on the coffee table from last night I guess. I sat down on the couch and stared at my phone. I didn't know what I was going to say if I called them. I'm just ready to get this over with.

I dialed my parents phone number; it was Saturday afternoon so they should be home. My dad finally picked up. I didn't know what to say.

"Who is Tanner Larson?" I heard the intake of breath, and I somehow knew it was true.

"He enlisted when you were 8, we never heard from him again. It was hard enough on us, and you loved your big brother. Eventually you just seemed to forget him, so we didn't tell you." My father was rambling and my mind felt like it was about to implode.

No. I didn't believe him. How could I just forget someone that I'd grown up with? It can't work that way. I could still hear my father on the other end of the phone, but I just couldn't do it right now. I pressed the red button and let the phone drop.

They lied to me.

You don't just forget your family. And you don't let your daughter forget her big brother. Suddenly, all my high school experiences flashed through my mind. If I had had a big brother to protect me, maybe it wouldn't have been so bad.

"Ahh" I jumped as I felt something hot clamp down on my shoulder. Reality came crashing back fast and I could feel the tears flowing down my face.

" Shh, it'll be okay." Kain whispered as he pulled me near him. Everything felt like it was moving, like everything I'd known was falling beneath my feet, but Kain was solid. He wasn't going to go anywhere, so I held onto him for dear life.

I don't know how long we sat like that, but I knew we couldn't stay here like this forever. I unwrapped my arms from around his waist where I'd been clinging and he seemed to get the hint and let me go as well. Wiping my tears away, I stood up and made my way to the door. I don't know where I plan on going, but it can't be here. He can't see me cry anymore. I have to fix myself.

"Carrie," I stopped because, for once, he called me Carrie, but I couldn't turn around, "where are you going?"

"I don't know." I wasn't sure if it was even an audible answer, but that's as good as he was going to get.

----Kain's POV----

I barely heard as she whispered, "I don't know," and walked out of the apartment. This was not good. I nearly had her ready mentally to go, this just blew all that to hell. What am I talking about, I'm sure getting mission cleared isn't anywhere near the top of her list. I needed to go see Morgon again.

As I made my way back to the office, I couldn't help but try to imagine what she was going through. As much as I tried, I couldn't. Everyone in my family was gone, and even if they weren't, they would never find me. I was on the last set of stairs to the office when Larson came into view, storming through the doors like the 5 year old he is. I did not foresee good things.

"You." He spat, his words seething with venom.

"Yep, the best and brightest, what can I do for you?" I knew being a smart ass to him probably wasn't a good idea right now, but would I really be me if I didn't?

"Ummf" That's probably a risk I should have taken. He had me shoved against the wall with his elbow pressing into my throat.

"Stay away from her if you know what's good for you. She's not going to be one of your little toys. I'm not done yet, she'll never be sent out." I could feel the grin spreading across my face.

"If I want her, she'll be mine by the end of the week." He suddenly released me, but he wasn't done. I knew the right hook was coming and I deserved it.

Copper. The way blood always tasted. She'd never be one of my 'toys,' she's way to good for that fate.

"Tandem, I will end you." And with that Larson disappeared down the stairs, hopefully never to be seen again. Sadly, that probably wasn't going to happen. He was mad.

Wiping the blood off my lip, I passed through the oak door to see that the room had become empty since my previous visit.

"She knows." I directed my statement to Morgon. He knew what I was talking about. The look of distress on his face said that much. After a few deep breathes he finally began to speak.

"It was bound to happen eventually. Where is she now?"

"I don't know, she dropped her phone and left. Said she didn't know where she was going. This just back stepped any progress I've made with her."

"We both know it won't take long for you to get her back. We need her here, for more than you realize. First and foremost, I got your yearly shrink evaluation back today. They aren't letting me send you on any more cleans until you have a partner. So you need her now too."

"You're kidding me. Those people are just wanna-be doctors that couldn't get their licenses, and you are going to let them run this business. My business."

"No Tandem, quite the contrary, I'm going to run my own business which you are a part of, and I happen to agree with them. You've been getting more reckless the closer you think you are to Them. Now, I need you to find her and make her trust you. I've had a job come up and I need to send you two out."

"Fine, but what is Larson doing back anyways? He's never going to agree to me working with her."

"He completed his orders in Iraq, there's no reason for him to be there anymore. He needs some downtime, so we put him on the board. Also, he doesn't have to agree to you working with Carisma, the vote already passed. I'll need you both on the plane by 5 pm, so you have about two hours to get her ready"

"Yes, sir"

Life just got a lot more complicated. Since the board already approved, the only person that can take Carisma off the active list is Morgon or myself. Neither of us is going to, so Larson is about to get really annoying. Now, if I were a girl, where would I go?

----Carrie's POV----

I walked.

It had been awhile and I'm not sure how far I'd walked, but it was starting to get cold. I debated going back to the dorms, but I'm not really ready to be indoors. I need this openness, I feel like I can breathe again.

I was strolling along the old cross-country track. No one was out at this time. I decided I would just sit here. I just wanted to be somewhere free, I felt like my world was collapsing and all I wanted to be doing was sitting.

"You know there are some places that you can see the sky and be warm." I hadn't heard Sadie jog up behind me.

"I'm not sure what happened, but people are talking. I'm not going to ask, but if you want to talk I'm here for you, just so you know." She said as she took a seat beside me in the dirt.

Staring off into the sky, I could almost pretend everything was normal.

After what seemed like forever, Sadie finally stood up.

"I think you should probably come in now. Its freezing out here, you are going to get sick."

Now that I thought about it, I was a little chilly, but it wasn't anything too horrible.

"I think I'll stay. But you should go in if your cold, I don't want to get you sick."

It wasn't long before I heard her steps fading into the distance. I let myself fall back onto the ground. I didn't even know what I was thinking about. The shock made me numb and impervious to the cold.

I had a brother. This whole time and they kept it from me. So did he. Tanner's insane if he thinks I'm going to turn away from this job because he doesn't want me to. Oh quite the contrary, ha I'm about to have one helluva time.

----Kain's POV----

"She's out on the track, by the bridge." Sadie said as I came out of the dorm. I'd looked everywhere for her.

"Thanks" I replied as I took off towards the track.

I knew she wouldn't take this well. Tanner just had to throw that in her face. God he doesn't think about anything. This is why they took us off the last project we worked together. Larson likes to storm in and shoot the place up, while I'm content to just sit back and calculate my shot down to one target. Less stress, less mess.

As I came up to the track, I could see her making her way across the muddy grass in the heals she had worn to the meeting. It looked sad and I got the sudden urge to carry her back to my apartment and hold her until everything in her world was okay again.

"When do we leave?" She asked, stopping abruptly. I was not expecting that. I was expecting her to hate this place, and then I'd have to talk her out of it as she was packing her bags.

"Are you sure you want to go on this?"

"We both know I don't really have an option, but yes, I am positive. How long do I have to pack?"

"You have about thirty minutes, then we are going to have to leave for the plane."

"Good, then let's go." With that she continued back the way I had come towards the dorm.

She was definitely a girl on a mission tonight. This was either going to be really good or really bad.

----Carrie's POV----

By the time I'm done today, I'm going to be so much of an asset to this organization that nothing Tanner does will get me thrown out. As for Tanner, well I'm about to be the absolute worst little sister possible.

I went into my room and quickly threw some clothes in a bag. Leather body suit (I thought someone randomly left it in my closet when I moved in, but now I'm guessing it wasn't an accident.) Black, knee high boots with an adorable 3 inch heal. Ugg, I guess I'll throw in the black Puma sneakers too. It's a really good thing I like this color otherwise this job would suck.

As I turn to leave I noticed my hair was a mess. Checking my watch, I still had about twenty-five minutes left, so I grabbed my comb and brushed it through then ratted it at the top for a little volume.

Perfect. Just then my phone rang.

Mason.

"What?"

"Geez, Sorry I called."

"No, I'm sorry Mason, I'm just in a hurry trying to get some stuff together. What do you need?"

"Don't go."

"What are talking about Mace?" I tried to fake amusement in my voice.

"I know where you're going. And you can't go. She'll be there. She's ready to end him now like she tried to end me. If you get in the way, you'll be gone too."

"What are you talking about, did Tanner put you up to this?"

"No, I haven't talked to Tanner in years."

"Who is 'She'?"

"It doesn't matter just promise me you won't go."

"Ugg, fine! I promise. Bye."

With that I hung up the phone. What the heck is going on? Dang, fifteen minutes, I have to get back to Kain so we can make the plane on time. I took off sprinting down the hall, through the stairs, and out to the front where Kain was waiting. He looked a little impatient.

"Sorry! Mason called, which I need to ask you about, but it can wait for later when we are on the plane. Let's go." I said as I slipped on my aviators and made my way towards his Vanquish.

"That's not the right way." Kain yelled.

"I'm going to the car."

"I know, but we don't need to take the car."

"Fine, which way?"

"Up."

I'm sure my face was like a neon sign of confusion. But, nevertheless, I silently followed Kain back into the building. He went straight for the stairwell.

"This goes up to Morgon's office."

"I know," he suddenly stopped on the sixth floor landing and turned towards me, "Are you positive you want to do this?"

"If I have to tell you yes one more time..."

"You'll do what? Honey, we both know you can't hurt me."

"Watch me."

"We'll see about that." He chuckled, and once again we marched our way up to the thirteenth floor.

When we reached the door on the thirteenth floor, Kain pushed through it and proceeded into the foyer outside of Morgon's office.

"Look around." He said staring at me, "Look closely."

Not sure what I was looking for, I glanced across everything in the small area. If I had blinked, I would have missed it. Right across from the big oak doors of Morgon's office, on the dark wood walls was a small circle of silver. I walked over to it and pressed on it. Out slid a small handle, which I pulled and along with it came a portion of the "wall."

"Congratulations," Kain said from behind me, I hadn't noticed him get so close, "now I believe we have a plane to catch."

Behind the door was one final staircase, which came to an end at a reinforced steel door.

"Now, I'll show you how it works this time." With that Kain stepped in front of me and placed his hand on a square on the wall beside the door, about eye level.

Click.

The door swung open to reveal a landing base, with a helicopter waiting to take us away to some place that I probably should have asked about before.

"Wow, is this always here?"

"Nope it only lands under the cover of dark, and as you can tell, it's not easy just to stumble upon it while wondering the dorm."

"Right."

"Are you going to get in the helicopter someday?" I guess I hadn't noticed what was going on, but I was able to see the stars plain as day up here and I must have gotten lost in them.

"Sorry." I said as I climbed up into the last remaining seat.

"No problem Miss, I'm Fred and I'll be your pilot this lovely morning, and this here is Charlie, my copilot." Introduced the men in the front seat.

"Oh, um, nice to meet you." It just kind of struck me how different this life was going to be from the normal life most teenage girls led. When they were worrying about which boy they liked, who they'd slept with last week when they were drunk, and what college to go to, I'd be checking who was next on the hit list.

"So what were you saying earlier about Mason calling?"

Right, I'd nearly forgot about that.

"He called me while I was packing, and he sounded I guess, umm, panicky? He said not to go, that she was ready to end him like she tried to end him. Basically, if I came with you I'd get caught up in it and be gone too."

"Who is She?"

"I don't have any idea, he said it didn't matter. I asked him if Tanner put him up to it and he told me he hadn't talked to Tanner in years. Why is that?"

"A few months after I got here Larson was sent into a deep cover op in Iraq, and now he's completed his task. Whenever an agent is sent to a job like that the shrinks always keep them inactive for an evaluation period upon return."

"Have you ever had to do a shrink evaluation?"

"Yep, we all do. But personally, I am one of their little pet projects. Which is why you're here. They won't let me back in the field without backup. I only trust what I know, and I know I have trained you, well more so directed you, in the right direction. I wasn't lying in there when I told them you were pretty much field ready from the start."

"Thanks, I think. So the only reason I'm here is because you couldn't get back to your job without me?"

"Honestly, yeah. I wouldn't have done it if I didn't trust your abilities. I'm reckless, but I'm not a masochist."

"You're reckless? That doesn't seem like you should be allowed within fifty feet of a firearm."

"Ha, are you crazy? I'm the best. Once I reach my goal though, I'm out. Done."

"A goal. Do you have a dream body count or something?"

"Killing isn't fun. Watching the light disappear from their eyes as the scope fills with red... Sorry, you don't want to hear this. "

"Yeah, actually I do want to hear this. If I'm going to be doing this on my own, I don't want to know the sugar coated code words of my job description."

"True, but you're just here for back up. There will be no shooting for you today. Hell, I'm not sure yet if you'll even get out of the car."

"What? No way. That is not fair."

"Just read the file. I don't feel like having this argument right now." And here I thought we were actually making progress.

I looked at the red-tape-lined file Kain had thrown in my lap. Inside were photos and what looked like reports. The first photo was, I guess, the equivalent of a mug shot, but it looked as if it had been cropped out of the family Christmas card. This was only given away by the cheesy smile and reflection of a decorated tree in the lens of his glasses. The next two photos were of a man stepping out of car, but he was looking the opposite way of the camera. A Toyota Corolla 180i to be exact, clearly a family car. The final two photos were nearly identical; I almost thought it was a mistake. However in the first photo, our guy had a brown package sitting in front of him on the table, while his blonde hair, blue eyed guest had a black metal briefcase. In the second photo, the two items had switched possession.

"Don't bother with the photos. Read the report; commit his physical markers to memory from that. Once you start looking at the photos you see him as more than a potential terrorist that we have been sent to eliminate."

"A potential terrorist?"

"Yeah, that briefcase contained the final engage switch for a suspected bomb."

"We are about to kill this man over suspicion? No, we can't do that. It's not right."

"James Whittleman. 34 years old. United States citizen, but has been a legal resident of Liechtenstein for the past six years. The engage switch in that case, completely harmless. That is until you look at the bigger picture. In the last five years the National Security Administration has been tracking purchases of Mr. Whittleman. Thanks to an overzealous science experiment in high school that nearly blew up his small town somewhere in Utah like a nuclear reactor, which earned him a permanent spot on the chemical watch list. He thought that by moving out of the states he could buy chemicals under the radar without their knowledge. He was wrong. Experts at the NSA that were given the purchase list that was put together agreed that all these ingredients could create a bomb big enough to literally remove Florida from the continental United States. I understand that's still just conjecture, but with this theory the NSA was able to turn his previous assembly partner, who confirmed that Mr. Whittleman was building a bomb in his backyard. Oh, and his wife and children went missing not long after that Christmas portrait was taken."

I didn't know what to say. I'm pretty sure my parent's house had everything you would need to make a small pipe bomb, but they weren't. I guess this difference is that the parts James Whittleman has lying around his house don't make a little pipe bomb.

"Are we just choosing between us and them?"

"What?"

"You know. We're stopping him before he can stop us. It's child's play really."

"Never thought of it that way, but yeah, it is. We have to be first."

"Awesome, we have become toddlers with guns. Who do you think 'She' is?"

"No clue. Mason got pulled because he returned from an operation that had gone wrong in France. It took awhile but Morgon finally let me in on what had happened. He was captured, tortured, I don't know the details, but he said the last person he saw was Evelyn walk down the stairs to where he was being held. Supposedly she asked someone why he was still conscious. It's totally ridiculous. Evelyn was in England and took an overnight ferry to go rescue him. "

"If that's what you think…"

"What? You believe him?"

"I didn't mean to say that out loud. I'm not saying I believe him, but if anyone at Elite was going to be one of the bad guys, it'd definitely be Evelyn."

"Right, I think someone just has some hard feelings over the stitches in her face."

"Jerk."

"Whatever. Just sleep, you aren't going to have another chance until we're on our way home."

Now that I think about it, I was pretty tired. I don't remember when the last time I slept was. Staring at the water below, I drifted into sleep thinking of what we were walking into that Mason was so afraid of.

"Mr. Whittleman, please talk to us. You don't want to do this. If you hit that trigger we're all going to blow up."

James was shaking, and you could see the confliction in his eyes. It wasn't supposed to happen this way. He wasn't supposed to see us, and he definitely wasn't supposed to have the bomb already assembled.

"James, think of the two toddlers next door, they'll go down with us."

"I am trying to take down an entire country, do you really think two imbeciles are going to stop me?"

It was like the world was suddenly playing in slow motion. I swear I could almost see the nerve response traveling from his brain, down his arm, through his fingers, and almost jump from his body to the trigger.

"No!" It was already too late.

Ughhh, it felt like a semi was slamming into me going a thousand miles an hour. I felt the wall of the house next door, but of course it didn't stop me. I continue to travel along a path along with all the debris and shrapnel that this area has become. The light was practically blinding, not even closing my eyes could block out the horrible shine.

The floor came and it felt like the world itself had attacked me.

"Ahhh!" The agony and pain was unbearable.

"Carrie, Carrie, wake up! What's wrong baby, wake up." I could feel the shaking and it took me a few seconds to get my bearings.

"What? I'm sorry. I was having a bad dream. Sometimes I get a little lost in it."

"It's fine. What was it about?"

"Oh, um, I fell out of the plane. I know, lame." I knew Kain would flip if he knew what I had really been dreaming about.

"These seatbelts are industrial grade, you're not going to go anywhere."

"How long was I out?"

"You mean before the blood-curdling scream? About three or four hours I'd guess. We're going to be landing in a few minutes anyways."

I took a deep breath.

"So this is it. How long will it take us?"

"We'll be in travel for about an hour and a half each way. The hit itself will probably take about two or three hours."

"We're taking it down now kids. As usual, Mr. Tandem, your car is on the runway, stocked and loaded."

"Fred, you know to call me Kain. I'll see you guys in a few hours."

"We'll be waiting" Charlie replied.

Jumping down from the helicopter, I saw a car waiting for us. It was exactly like Kain's car back in the states, but there is no way it got here before us.

"What's the Vanquish doing here?"

"It's not my Vanquish. Well it is, but it's not the one I keep in the states. It stays in storage in various countries, and gets shipped ahead. Fully stocked with every weapon that could possibly be needed."

Liechtenstein. We had passed city lights awhile back, and now everything just looked plain. Kain didn't say anything, I suppose it's because he wasn't used to having company, and I had no idea what to say. So it was a silent ride.

In the dash was a touch screen panel. Currently it showed a coordinate grid with a little blinking light in the center I guess that was us. I felt the car slow down.

"What are we doing?"

"We're about ten miles out, so we have to get the weapons ready. You can take the silver Smith & Wesson, I'll take the black." He said throwing me a gun.

"Here's the silencer, attach it to the muzzle and load it, the bullets should be under your seat."

I stuck my hand under the seat. Ick. I hate reaching into dark places when I don't know what's there. I felt the cardboard box, and yanked it out.

"Problems?" I hate when he watches me.

"Not at all."

I loaded the clip and slid it back in the gun. I screwed the silencer on and laid the gun in my lap.

This seemed like as good a time as any for my aviators, so I hid my eyes behind as we took off towards our target.

"So how are we going in? The driveway?"

"Pretty much. He hires an escort service, its time for his purchase to be delivered and so the call was intercepted and your information was given."

"My information? I don't think he should know my information."

"Physical markers, Carisma. Also, you're temporary name is Sabrina Charm. I'll walk you up to the door as a guard and to collect the payment. Then it'll be over."

"Sounds easy."

"They usually are."

The driveway was short and secluded. The Vanquish came to a stop.

"Heat sensing cameras on the house says there's only one person inside. Our target."

"Okay, well I think its time to die."

"Yeah, I think." He gave me a look. Whatever, I ignored it and opened the car door.

"Hey your..." Kain start to warn me about my gun, but I wasn't dumb I slipped it into my waistband as I was standing. Absolutely no way Whittleman could see it from inside the house.

I listened to the gravel crunch under my stilettos as we approached the door.

The porch was cute; it almost looked like his family could still be living here, and any minute they'd come running up for lemonade. Kain pressed the doorbell.

"Excuse yourself to the bathroom as soon as possible."

The door opened just then.

He looked exactly like the picture. I decided I'd go ahead and play the part to it's fullest. Good thing I left my hair down today. I grabbed a strand and started twirling it around my index finger. I even licked my lips once or twice.

"James Whittleman I presume. I have Sabrina here, and as you know, she's one of our more high earning girls so company policy mandates I be by the bedroom door. Just securing assets you understand."

"Of course, let me go get the cash real fast." He said eyes roaming my body.

"Umm, excuse me Mr. Whittleman, but do you have a bathroom or bedroom I can freshen up in?" I needed to make sure he was ahead of me when I stepped into the house, or he'd see the gun.

"I sure do, darling. First door on the left is the bedroom, you'll see the attached bathroom as soon as you walk in."

"The money sir." Kain interrupted, clearly trying to intimidate Whittleman into taking off before me. It worked.

"Oh right." With that he took off down the hall towards a large open area that looked like a living room.

Kain and I stepped in and I hurried to the door.

"Stay in there until I come get you."

"Got it."

Just like he said, the bathroom was right there. I walked in and locked the door behind me. Pressing myself against the wall opposite the door, I waited.

One minute and thirteen seconds.

Bang.

Bang.

Heart and head. Any good assassin goes for both. At least that's what Kain says, and it must be true. He's one of, if not the, best.

"Sabrina, it's security, you can come out now." Kain was knocking at the door.

Nevertheless, I wasn't going to take a chance. With the gun by my side, I flipped the lock and on the count of three yanked the door open, while at the same time raising my gun prepared to shoot whoever was on the other side of the door. Just in case it wasn't Kain.

"Perfect." Kain actually smiled at the fact that I had a gun pressed to his chest. I put it back in the waist of my pants and we left the house.

----One hour later----

The car ride was nearly unbearable. The mood just seemed somber. We were about thirty minutes from the helicopter when I decided to play with the stereo. A car like this had to have one right?

I tried the touch screen panel in the dashboard. Yep, that was it. A bunch of squares popped up, kind of like an iPod and there was music. Dance playlist. Yep, that's what we need.

Bottoms up. This song was perfect for just insane dancing. And that's what I intend to do.

"What are you doing?" Kain yelled over the music.

"Jamming out to the music silly, you should try it." I said with my arms in the air, rolling my body in strange ways due to being in a car and all.

"I can't silly," he said sarcastically, "I'm driving."

Next song up on the stereo was Love like Woe, which I love. It's adorable.

I probably should have thought this through, but I didn't. I got in Kain's face, bad idea. Our eyes locked.

"You could do a lot of things while driving if you really wanted."

Not even three seconds later his lips were on mine. Then I felt his arm wrap around my waist and pull me onto his lap.

We are driving, well he is. In a car. This is not good.

"This isn't what I had in mind when I said that."

"What? Does Carisma not trust me?" He smirked at me.

"I trust you with my life." It was true. If I didn't I wouldn't have flown to this foreign country with him at a moments notice.

"Then you know you'll be fine." And he kissed me again.

I opened my eyes for a split second and saw him glance at the road before reaching over to the panel.

As much trust as was occurring in this car, it really needed to stop soon. I believed in fate, and we were tempting it way too much for one night.

I broke away and looked into his eyes once more before crawling back into my seat and stared out the window. It was dark now and I could see the stars more clearly than I ever have before.

His eyes. When I looked into them, they were so deep. They seemed to go on forever. The walls weren't there, and it was absolutely beautiful.

I looked back over at him. His hair was messed up, which made me laugh. I hid it with a smile and glanced down at his hand, which was resting on the console between our seats.

Why not?

I reached over and slowly put my hand in his, then went back to looking at my stars. It didn't take long at all for him to enclose my hand in his. In a strange way, just being like this, everything felt safe.

"Oh shit."

"What? Oh..." We were driving down the runway and up ahead was our helicopter...engulfed in red and orange flames. Smoke was billowing skyward, looking like one of those horrible clouds that bring a downpour.

Something was definitely wrong, and I got the feeling it wasn't done.

The Vanquish came to a stop, about as close as we could get to the flames. As we stepped out of the car I slipped the gun I'd had earlier back in my waistband.

"What's going on Kain?"

Suddenly there was a horrid laugh from the direction of the smoke. Almost as if on cue, a gust of wind came by washing away the smoke. In the clearing, someone was walking towards us.

"Maybe you should have listened to Mason little girl. Now you'll have to disappear with my sweet baby."

"What the hell Evelyn?" Kain yelled, rage evident in his voice.

"You know as well as I do Kain, we don't do this dirty work just so we can give ourselves a pat on the back at the end of the day for eliminating another bad guy. We all have ulterior motives, some are a little more power based than others."

"You did this for power? What kind of power did you get from burning up a helicopter?" I questioned.

"The helicopter had nothing to do with it, but our dear friends Fred and Charlie were starting to piece together the pieces of phone conversation that took place on their planes. Turns out they lace those jets with unregistered microphones that not even Morgon knows about."

"Oh my god, they were still in there." I whispered. Kain was now standing right beside me, and his hand grabbed mine, lacing our fingers together in order to pull me slightly behind him.

"So, what power is killing all these people going to get you?"

"Oh you blind little boy. Cardinal. Once you're gone, it's all mine. As soon as the threat of you is eliminated, I'll be moved to the head of it, and since we have prominent placing in most European governments, it won't be long before we overthrow America. I'm quite bored with this useless chatter..."

Bang. There wasn't time to do anything. The gun came out of nowhere.

I felt Kain drop beside, as the tears of realization and pain streamed out of my eyes.

"Ahh!" I was crying like a baby. I could hear the steps she took as she walked towards us. Pressure, there had to be pressure on a wound.

"There's no use, once I put a bullet through your pretty little head you won't be able to save him anyways." Evelyn laughed again.

"Kain stay with me. Look at me. It's going to be okay baby I promise." He looked at me, our eyes locked once again.

"I'm…I'm so sorry," He started to cough, "You shouldn't…not be in this. I was…selfish to bring you out." Breathing was hard on him. Every sweet breath brought the aftertaste of pain.

"No, I'm ready." With that I reached for the gun, pulled it out as I switched off the safety, swung it level with her heart, and pulled the trigger.

Bang.

She crumbled to the ground.

The first scar. The first life I'd taken. The rain came pouring down as I sat with Kain, staring into his eyes; silently begging him not to bring on the pain that speaking came with.

"Kain we're going to be fine, okay, stay with me." I put pressure on his gunshot; luckily Evelyn was a terrible shot and seemed to have missed any organs.

I grabbed his phone from his pocket and dialed the one person who would know what to do.

"Morgon," A crack of lightening filled the air, "Kain's been shot."

FSC
www.fsc.org
MIX
Papier | Fördert
gute Waldnutzung
FSC® C083411

Zeitfracht Medien GmbH
Ferdinand-Jühlke-Straße 7
99095 Erfurt, Deutschland
produktsicherheit@kolibri360.de

Druck:
CPI Druckdienstleistungen GmbH
im Auftrag der
Zeitfracht Medien GmbH
Ein Unternehmen der Zeitfracht - Gruppe
Ferdinand-Jühlke-Str. 7
99095 Erfurt